D1479101

MRS FITZWILLIAM DARCY

And Other Stories

Anne Fafoutakis

UPFRONT PUBLISHING
LEICESTERSHIRE

MRS FITZWILLIAM DARCY *And Other Stories*
Copyright © Anne Fafoutakis 2001

All Rights Reserved

ISBN 1 84426 011 9

First Published 2001 by
MINERVA PRESS

Second Edition 2002 by
UPFRONT PUBLISHING
Leicestershire

MRS FITZWILLIAM DARCY
And Other Stories

Friends and Relations

In some ways, Mark Bascombe had had what is called 'a good war'. Mentioned in dispatches, then awarded a DFC, he had, miraculously for a pilot in the Royal Flying Corps, come out of it all relatively unscathed. Of course, there were the nights when he'd wake up sweating and shaking, but that was only to be expected. Many flyers experienced ghastly nightmares in which their plane was on fire and there was no way out. Living alone, he had no one to turn to when he awoke. In 1914, his fiancée, Rhoda, had offered her services as a nurse at a military hospital in Sussex. In 1917, while Mark was serving in France, she had written to break off their engagement. A blinded officer of the Black Watch had come to depend on her, and she had resolved to dedicate the rest of her life to 'being his eyes' as she put it. 'He needs me, Mark. I'm sure you'll understand...'

And I don't need you, I suppose? he thought ruefully. What if I were to be blinded in the middle of a dogfight? He soon saw the absurdity of the idea, since landing an aircraft in a situation like that would be impossible.

Mark was one of the few to have survived the carnage from start to finish. After the Armistice, someone said, 'Let me tell you, Bascombe, a lot of chaps prayed they'd be flying in your wing. They reckoned you led a charmed life.' Perhaps so.

Once, on leave, he had visited Rhoda, at her request, and met her husband. He was a tall, handsome Scot with hair of burnished gold and such a gentle manner that it was hard to picture him charging at the enemy with a bayonet. But his Military Cross was no illusion and he had earned it at great cost to his future. The two men hit it off very well and when, at one point, Rhoda was called away, Ian turned in Mark's direction.

'You know, Bascombe, Rhoda has given me the will to live. I had quite decided not to carry on for I could see no future except a constant dependency on others.' He smiled. 'Funny how often one uses the word "see", especially when one can't. Anyway, I was determined not to ruin her life, especially when I found out she was engaged. But Matron came to see me and gave me hell.

Rhoda had gone to her in tears, saying she felt a total failure and wanted to give up nursing altogether. "Well," said Matron, "I'm having none of that! I'm not going to lose an excellent nurse because of some petulant Scot!" Matron is a formidable woman. I wish I could see what she looks like.'

'Formidable is what she looks like,' said Mark, laughing. 'But seriously, Ian, have no misgivings about Rhoda and me. In any case, a flyer has no business making demands on his nearest and dearest.'

'I don't want pity, Mark.'

'That's the very last thing Rhoda has in mind. There's no hypocrisy in her make-up. I've known her since we were children and she was never able to hide her feelings, good or bad. With you, she is a happy woman.'

Mark left the hospital certain that Rhoda and Ian would make a success of their marriage, despite the odds… or even perhaps because of them. Also, he found much to his relief that the bitterness and resentment were no longer eating him. The RFC was still in the embryonic stage and several of his colleagues had received 'Dear John' letters. Putting it bluntly, they were considered too much of a risk.

By 1917, spirits were at a low ebb, so that when America entered the war and the Lafayette Escadrille came over, it brought a welcome breath of fresh air. With the arrival of the 'Yanks' – as the British would persist in calling them, much to the annoyance of the southerners – things changed. The Americans were breezy, very young and equipped with crisp new uniforms and crisp new aircraft. Mark struck up a friendship with one Jeb Hoskins, a 6ft 5in giant from Williamsburg, Virginia.

What singled him out from most of his countrymen was his insatiable curiosity and his interest in everything. He was even fascinated by naval engagements, and mentioned the Battle of the Falklands. Mark was amazed.

'Well, it was in the papers, you know.'

'I hope they got it right and it didn't suffer in the translation.'

'Correct me if I'm wrong, then. On 8 December 1914, a strong British squadron went on the warpath. Er, that's Red

Indian for going out of your way to make trouble. Anyway, it seems that in November, five German cruisers had wiped out Admiral Cradock's squadron at Coronel, in Chile. Well, this Admiral Von Spee, flying his flag on *Scharnhorst*, rounded the Horn, confident that Germany ruled the waves. But your Admiral Sturdee soon disabused him of that idea. He sank four of the five ships. *Dresden* got away, only to be sent to the bottom three months later. The Germans lost two thousand men.'

'And the British, six.'

'I'm sorry. Was I showing off? I tend to when I'm spouting history.'

'The reason I know is that my sister's eldest son was one of the six. You know, Jeb, you ought to be a teacher. You make history come alive. What are you planning to do after the war?'

Jeb grinned. 'Teach! That's what I have a degree in History for.'

Hoskins was indeed full of surprises. Once, when he had three days' leave or, as he called it, furlough, he went walkabout. On his return, the sentry at the gate could only gasp, for Hoskins was not alone. He was towing a rope at the other end of which were three German soldiers tied to each other.

'Where do I go with these, Corporal?' he drawled.

The man stammered that he was sure he didn't know, sir. What was sir's password, if sir pleased? Hoskins obliged, then handed over his charges to two mechanics, who took them straight to the Adjutant. Later, Hoskins was called in to see him.

'Well, young man,' said Captain Bennett, 'what am I supposed to do with your three beauties?'

Hoskins seemed fascinated by the shine on his boots.

'Sit down, man. You're not being court-martialled, you know – not yet, anyway.'

Hoskins eased his bulk into the chair facing the desk. Captain Bennett regarded him with considerable interest, then said, 'As a matter of fact, we are now in the happy position of knowing something of the morale of our opponents. It seems the Germans have been under the impression that, like them, our forces have been on almost a starvation diet. Actually, the British army has better provisions than anyone else. If we've had to leave the field in a hurry, the Germans have found there luxuries they could only dream of. This deception practised by their superiors has broken many a spirit and some of them see little reason to continue the fight. All this we found out thanks to you.'

'That would explain their eagerness to surrender. I didn't force them, sir.'

'Quite. But don't make a habit of it, will you Hoskins? This is an airfield. We're really not equipped to process prisoners of war.'

Apart from his entertainment value, which was considerable, Hoskins was solid, reliable, a true friend and a born flyer. He could make that crate of his do anything but fry an omelette and sing *Madame Butterfly*. He looked after it, babied it and made sure no one could fly *Ermintrude* during his leave by making her unserviceable in ways known only to himself – and *Ermintrude*. Mark wanted Hoskins to survive this war more than anyone else he knew. This was a young man worth something and he was certain that if they ever did come through the carnage, they would be friends for life. Indeed, following the Armistice, they corresponded regularly and, in 1920, the young American came to London.

The motive was pure Hoskins. He had heard about the Unknown Warrior and was determined to see the ceremony. Although there had been a certain amount of secrecy surrounding the event, Mark was really not at all surprised that Hoskins knew. He had a way with him which inspired confidence and people would tell him everything. He would have been a treasure in the Intelligence Service. He knew that the original idea had come from a young army chaplain serving in France who had seen too many men for whom a proper funeral had not been possible. Perhaps England could honour them by singling out one of their number to whom the nation could pay homage.

'And he's to be placed in the Cenotaph,' Hoskins concluded.

'No, Jeb, it's now to be Westminster Abbey. In three days' time.'

Accordingly, on the eleventh of November, the two friends arrived at Whitehall for what was to be for Hoskins the experience of a lifetime.

Set a little apart from the Cenotaph was a mute witness – the gun carriage bearing the coffin of the Unknown Warrior draped with the Union Jack. Presently the official party arrived, headed by King George V accompanied by Field Marshal Haig. When the monarch unveiled the new memorial, which replaced the wooden one erected in 1919, the assembled crowd could only marvel at its simplicity. Sir Edwin Lutyens, the architect, had deliberately omitted any religious symbols, for he reasoned that the 800,000 commemorated were of many different beliefs and some of no beliefs at all. The legend, 'To our Glorious Dead', said it all.

Hoskins whispered, 'It's magnificent. Is it marble?'

'No, it's Portland Stone, the purest white.'

The King now turned towards the gun carriage and placed a wreath on top of the flag-draped coffin. Then the procession made its way to the Abbey, the King, as honorary pall-bearer, following close behind. Not being of the official party, Mark and Jeb had to wait until the ceremony was over. When they entered later, the sight caused Hoskins to catch his breath. The coffin, surrounded by floral tributes, was guarded by four sentries from each of the services standing on each corner, arms reversed and heads bowed.

'It's all so quiet, so dignified. I never realised what an important role silence plays in something like this. I wish I knew more about the Unknown Warrior... how he was selected, I mean. The papers were so vague.'

A young naval officer standing behind them now stepped forward.

'Excuse me, but I gather from your accent you're American.'

Hoskins held out a hand and introduced himself. 'Lieutenant...?'

'Grahame. Michael Grahame, Royal Navy.' He turned to Mark.

'Mark Bascombe, late RFC. And my friend here was in the Lafayette Escadrille. We flew together during the war. Is there anything at all you can tell us about this? Hoskins is a great one for detail. You may find it hard to believe, but his main reason for coming over was today's ceremony. Any enlightenment will be much appreciated.'

The naval officer had noticed that people were turning to look at them and realised this was not the place for long conversations.

'It might be better to talk somewhere else. But before we go, Hoskins, I should like to draw your attention to the floral tributes. The anchor of white flowers is from the Navy and the laurel wreath on the Union Jack is from the gardens of Ypres – what's left of them.'

They left the Abbey in silence and repaired to Mark's flat, which was not too far away. Once settled comfortably with a tankard of beer each, Hoskins turned to Grahame.

'I want to hear it all, or as much as you can tell me, anyway. My paper sent me over here especially for this.'

'So you're a journalist, are you, Hoskins?'

'Not really. I'm on a sabbatical before reporting to the university after Easter. So, how much do you know, Lieutenant?'

Michael Grahame related much of which Hoskins already knew, but the American listened in silence, leaning forward eagerly when the matter of the selection was broached.

'The idea was to choose a man whose identity would never be made public. In fact, the remains of several men from different battlefields were brought to a hut in St Pol – that's near Arras. They had been placed on stretchers, each covered with a Union Jack. At midnight, a Brigadier General was led to the hut and, eyes closed, he touched one of the stretchers. The officer then left the hut, his work done. The man selected was placed in a coffin and taken to Boulogne, where he was placed overnight in the chateau. The following morning – yesterday – after being saluted by Marechal Foch himself, the coffin was carried onto my ship, *Verdun*, where four sailors stood guard for the crossing. When we reached Dover, he was accorded a field marshal's salute – that's nineteen guns. I was lucky enough to be one of the six officers from the four services chosen to bear the coffin from the ship to the train. That's how I happen to have three days' leave.'

'I'd say we're the ones who are lucky – to have met you, eh, Jeb?'

The American, who had listened mesmerised, shook his head in disbelief. 'Grahame, you're the icing on the cake! How can I ever thank you?'

'Just send me a copy of the article you're going to write. And now I'd better be off or I shall miss my train.'

'I expect you're in a hurry to get back to your wife. Three days go by very fast.'

When Mark found out that Michael was not married, he insisted he stay on and show Jeb some historic sites. The idea met with great success as the three men found they had much in common. Mark also suggested that if he had some leave, Michael should spend Christmas in London.

On their return from seeing Michael off at the station, Mark found two very welcome letters. The first was from the solicitors to whom he had been articled before the war, offering him a position to start on the twentieth of February. This came as a great relief as his funds were running low. Although his parents had left him comfortably off and with a large flat, the money could only go so far. For two years he had been unable to find a job, like many other returning servicemen. Well, at last help was at hand and, best of all, it had been unsolicited. The other letter was from his sister, inviting him down to Surrey for Stella's eighteenth birthday party the following week. Knowing Hoskins would still be in London, he asked if he could bring him along. Janet, who knew about Hoskins, agreed.

On their way to Surrey in the train, Mark explained, 'Janet had what we would call a "bad war", Jeb. In the summer of 1914 she had a husband, two sons and a daughter. By the end of 1916, she had lost her husband in the Battle of the Somme, the eldest boy you already know about, and Robin at Gallipoli. Now there's only Stella.'

Once off the train they made their way to Jasmine Cottage and at first sight of it, Jeb could hardly contain himself. Here was a real English cottage, thatched roof and all. At this point the front door opened and Stella stood there. Jeb was poleaxed. Mark grinned.

'This is Jeb Hoskins, Stella. Your mother probably told you he was coming.'

Stella responded by giving Jeb her hand, which disappeared into his huge fist. When she stepped aside to let them pass, the American seemed rooted to the spot. Mark gave him a little push, telling him to mind his head. 'It's a cottage, Jeb. Careful!'

As they all went in, Janet emerged from the kitchen, kissed her brother and smiled warmly at Jeb. 'I've just this minute taken the scones out of the oven. I hope you're ready for some tea?'

Jeb laughed. 'Well, of course there would be tea. And scones. Perfect!'

Later, he asked to see the garden and Mark, who could see the way things were heading said, 'You've done enough work, Janet, giving us this delicious spread. Stella and I will clear up and you can show Jeb your garden. And be prepared to answer a lot of questions!'

At dinner that evening, the irrepressible young American enthused over the garden, Janet's cooking, Surrey – in fact everything but the one topic that was really exercising his mind: Stella. That night, he slept like a baby.

The following morning there were the preparations for the party. At one point Mark asked his sister if he and Jeb could be useful.

'How's the log situation, Janet? We can chop enough wood to last you till May.'

Jeb added, 'And if there's anything else – plumbing, electrics, carpentry – just say the word. Here we are, ready, willing and able. Right, Mark?'

'Right, Jeb. Though how much longer *you're* going to be able is questionable. Each time you move from room to room, you crack your head.'

'Well, I can also effect some modifications to the ceilings. I'm not just a pretty face, you know.'

Needless to say, the party went off beautifully and the time flew by. Mark reflected that in the few days they had been there, Jeb had succeeded beyond his wildest hopes. He had wanted him to be invited because he felt a new, breezy personality would cheer up his sister. The last time he had seen Janet, a year ago, he had been heartbroken at the change in her. When they were younger, she had always been the one with the looks: rosy cheeks, shining blue eyes and hair the colour of corn. But three deaths in a row had, of course, taken their toll. Now, within a few days of their visit, Jeb had brought such joy and laughter into the house that Janet was beginning to look more like her old self.

The night before they were due to return to London, matters took an interesting turn. Stella and Jeb were strolling in the garden and Janet said to Mark, 'I'd like to talk to you about Jeb. It's obvious you consider him a good friend and he seems extremely nice, but...'

'He's a first-rate chap.'

'But is he dependable? What do you really know of his background, his family? Is he perhaps engaged to some girl in America?'

'Why all the questions, Janet?'

'Well, to tell you the truth, he's asked for Stella's hand.'

'But that's wonderful! Stella will be the happiest girl in the world. She'll never find anyone better, I promise you. He's dependable, of excellent background; his father is Dean of the university where he is to teach next year. His mother died of the Spanish flu in 1917.'

'I thought that was only in Europe.'

'No, unhappily it went round the world. And no, to get back to your questions, he is not engaged or anything else. He's a very special young man, Janet.' As she frowned, he asked, 'What's wrong? Still not convinced?'

'Well, the thing is, he wants both of us to go back with him.'

'That's a marvellous idea.'

'But, Jasmine Cottage...'

'Holds too many memories. Janet, do be sensible. Stella was bound to get married and you'll never find a more splendid son-in-law. If he wants both of you to go back with him, the offer is genuine. He means it.'

Everything was arranged for a Christmas wedding. Jeb would stay on at Jasmine and then the three of them would leave for America before Easter. He had assumed Mark would be best man, but the offer was not accepted. As Stella had no father, it would be up to her uncle to give her away.

'But choose any of your friends and welcome.'

'You're the only friend I have here. I don't know anyone else...'

A second later the same thought struck them and they both cried out, 'Michael!'

Janet insisted that if Michael could get Christmas leave he should stay at Jasmine. Accordingly, a letter was dispatched that very day and in no time at all came the answer, in the affirmative.

Jeb and Stella were married on Boxing Day and, despite his unshakeable belief that sailors should not get married, Michael found he had fallen in love with one of the two bridesmaids. He fought the temptation tooth and nail but the whole atmosphere at Jasmine was so euphoric that he gave up the uneven struggle and proposed.

Perhaps if Rowena had turned him down, he would have given up the idea for ever; but she did not, and they settled on Valentine's Day, a few days before he was due to sail. The local vicar was being swamped with requests for banns to be read. He had never known anything like it. There was obviously something strange coming from the direction of Jasmine Cottage, for Mark had renewed a childhood friendship with Susanna Donaldson. One look at this beautiful bridesmaid and he was lost. He had no other choice but to propose and, happily, she said yes.

Thinking three wedding receptions might prove too much for Janet, he and Michael decided on a double wedding. Jeb and Stella would be back from their honeymoon and the three men would be a team again.

Matters proceeded apace. Jasmine Cottage was sold without difficulty – to Michael. This would be his very first property and, like most sailors, he was very proud of it. In a little over two years, he would be out of the Navy and able to settle permanently.

When Stella and Jeb returned from their honeymoon, Janet could see that her daughter was supremely happy. Mark told her about Susanna and nothing could have pleased her more.

'Mark, she's a wonderful girl and I know you'll be very happy.'

'Congratulations from me, too. Terrific news, Mark.'

'*Uncle* Mark, if you please. My God, you're the biggest nephew anyone ever inherited!'

'There's more news still,' Janet cut in. 'Jasmine Cottage has been sold, to Michael. He thought Rowena might like it.'

'Rowena? Oh, this is all unbelievable. I don't know what to say.'

'I do,' said Jeb. 'When I first saw Jasmine Cottage, I said it was enchanted and I was right. What do you put in those scones of yours, Janet?'

Valentine's Day dawned crisp and clear. Fortunately, the rain took the hint and did not dampen the spirits, or the dresses, of the two brides and their matron of honour. Jeb stood up for Mark, and Rowena's brother was Michael's best man. The brides were given away by their respective fathers and the little church at Borden was packed.

Michael and Rowena left immediately for Portsmouth, as he was to sail in a few days. Mark and Susanna went to London for their honeymoon and she was delighted with her new home.

A few weeks later, Stella, Jeb and Janet boarded the train that was to take them to Liverpool and their ship. Life had changed so dramatically for them all in such a short time. Three of the people he loved most in the world were leaving, probably for good, Mark thought. But at least Susanna would be there.

'I shall expect to hear from all of you very regularly,' he said.

'Yes, Uncle Mark.'

'Don't be impertinent, Junior. Mind your manners.'

It was clear to Janet that they were both struggling to hide their feelings. She wondered whether she would ever see Mark again, although he had promised if he could wangle a long leave, he would come to Virginia.

As the train finally moved off, Susanna said, 'Let's go home, Mark. Big day tomorrow.'

When he'd first reported for work in February, he'd been pleased to find that all his apprehensions had been unnecessary. Everyone at the office was most helpful and he realised he had not entirely forgotten what he had learnt there before the war. The big day Susanna mentioned was the first time that Mark was to be in court with his barrister, an exceptional honour for someone who had not been so long in chambers.

In fact, within three years, he was up for a partnership and all was right with his world. It was time to start a family. They wanted to catch up with the Grahames, who were now the happy parents of twins. Mark and Susanna went down to Jasmine Cottage for the christening, and a few months later, the Grahames were in London to return the compliment when Michael Jeb

Bascombe made his appearance.

Meanwhile, in America, the news was all propitious. In his spare time Jeb had succeeded in writing a best-seller based on his visit to England in 1920, when he had also managed to see Canterbury, Winchester and Stonehenge. He still taught and was, as may be imagined, a very popular professor. Taking on board what was, at that time, a novel idea, he initiated a crammer's. He had realised early on that Janet was not taking too kindly to a life of ease and that she missed her teaching, which she loved. Consequently, she was given an office in the Dean's residence where she could help those students who found it difficult to follow the more advanced history lectures.

For some time now, Dr Hoskins, Jeb's father – the Dean – had made a practice of dropping in to see her as she prepared to leave in the afternoons.

'Well, Janet. Finished for today, are you?'

'Yes, Philip, and it was most rewarding. It always is, as you must know.'

'Several students have come to see me to say how much you're helping them. You're giving them the confidence to pursue their studies when they thought they couldn't go on. It's a great gift you have, lady.'

'They're such delightful young people. So receptive.'

Dr Hoskins stayed longer than usual that afternoon. Not to put too fine a point to it, he asked her to be his wife. Janet was staggered. She hadn't seen it coming. She was flattered, to be sure, for he was an older version of his son and consequently a very special person. When he saw her hesitation, he tried to make light of it.

'You know, Janet, I suspect we're being groomed as potential babysitters. It would save a lot of time if we could operate as a team, don't you think?'

She was just about to speak when the door burst open and Jeb and Stella stood there.

'Well?' they both said, looking at Dr Hoskins.

'Not yet,' he said quietly. 'I'm working on it. Give me time.'

Janet cried, 'Everyone knew but me, is that it? Don't I count?'

'More than you'll ever know, my dear. But the children did so want you to say yes. And so do I.'

'But I did so want to see Mark and...' Her voice trailed off.

'And so you shall. I've nothing to do all summer and I'm determined to see Scotland and the Lake District. And the famous Jasmine Cottage, of course. I depend on you to tell me what to take with me—'

'An umbrella!' chorused Jeb and Stella, laughing.

In her heart of hearts Janet knew that she and Philip Hoskins would make 'a good team', as he had put it. How could she refuse such a delightful man?

Suddenly Stella said, 'You're going to be my mother-in-law, Mother.'

'And my mother-in-law and stepmother. Hey, is this legal?' asked Jeb.

'We'll have to consult the Bible. That tells you everything,' said the Dean.

Mark and Susanna were able to come over for the wedding and Mark gave his sister away, while Jeb stood as best man for his father. Then, Philip and Janet boarded the train for New York and their ship bound for England. The Bascombes came too, as they were anxious to go back to their son, whom they had left with the Grahames. Meanwhile, Rowena had heard from Stella that she would be coming to England for the christening of her own child, due in two months' time. The Grahames insisted that she and Jeb stay with them – for old times' sake.

Rowena's father had offered Michael a partnership in his firm so he had not been obliged to look for work elsewhere. It was good news all round.

Once the Hoskins family had arrived in force, the Bascombes came down for the christening. It was a riotous household, with three toddlers and a newborn baby boy; the vicar, who was still there, did them proud.

Later, when the toasts were being drunk, Mark raised his glass.

'I had always thought war was the worst thing that could happen to anyone. But if it hadn't been for the war, Jeb and I would never have met, Michael would not have approached us in the Abbey and we would not now be celebrating this wonderful day. I drink to you all, my nearest and my very dearest.'

Trina

Chapter One

At the beginning of the twentieth century, it was still possible to find a club where intellectuals could meet without thought of planning revolutions or assassinating the odd capitalist or grand duke. The Revolution was still some way off, as indeed was World War I – the so miscalled Great War; food riots and the elimination of Rasputin at a supper party had not yet happened.

St Petersburg was considered very elegant and had, at one time, served as the capital of Russia. It is the country's second most important city and has always tended to look towards the West – not like Moscow, which faces inward.

It was founded in 1703, and so was comparatively recent, and owed its existence and its name to one man – Peter the Great (1672–1725). He succeeded to the throne at the age of ten, and in 1721 was proclaimed Father of the Fatherland, Peter the Great and Emperor of all Russia.

When he visited Europe, it had a lasting effect on him. He secretly despised the fine ladies he saw. How small they must have seemed to him – he stood 6ft 7in! But to his credit, he did have a receptive mind and took up new trades eagerly, showing a great talent for carpentry. By the time they embarked at Amsterdam for Archangel, the Russian party was 640 strong. Peter's first act on his return was to cut off the beards of the nobility – the West had arrived!

Realising that the only hope for Russian expansion was to obtain seaports, his ambition stretched to the shores of the Baltic and the Black Sea. He shifted the capital from Moscow to Ingria – his newly acquired Baltic territory – and built St Petersburg. Always keen to try something new, he encouraged the use of stone in building, reasoning it would not catch fire as did wood. He founded academies of arts and sciences, introduced universal taxation, and built schools and hospitals. He brought in French and Italian architects who were lavish with his money and also a trifle cavalier where human lives were concerned. (Forced labour had been imported from every part of Russia.) It has to be admitted that a magnificent, classical city was the result. There were palaces and museums – the Hermitage is, of course, the best-known example today – and the Winter Palace.

On the Nevski Prospect, the most famous street in the city, was the aforementioned men's club. It was said that their table was without equal, combining as it did all that was best in Russian, French and Italian cuisine.

The organisation was based on the European model and the members were treated with the greatest courtesy and addressed by name – correctly!

On this particular evening, we shall eavesdrop on three gentlemen, each one different from his fellows. They have enjoyed a superb dinner and are now seated at a smaller table for their coffee and liqueurs. One of them has been holding forth for an inordinate length of time.

Yascha Mounine is a Councillor who used to be a merchant. He has found the 'fringe benefits' of the Civil Service greatly to his liking; he is intensely mercenary, but will deny it on oath, maintaining he is merely realistic. To compensate for a certain lack of intelligence, he has substituted cunning.

His mouth, when not gainfully employed in eating, talking or puffing at a cigar, is almost permanently open, giving the impression that the spring has broken; his staccato voice is rather unattractive, and not one to be lived with for more than a few minutes. He has a fine figure and chooses to make capital of it: he has discovered a tailor who imports fine English cloth, and naturally he makes sure his circle of acquaintances know all about it!

The dashing young captain on his left, Alexei Terkov, has the kind of face that invites trust, and in fact, he is open in all his dealings. He is clearly of excellent family and puts up with Mounine not only because of his curiosity value, but also because they happen to be neighbouring landowners in the country. Alexei is a confirmed optimist, and his happy manner shines through everything he says or does; which may explain why he cannot understand Mounine's habit of looking on the dark side of everything.

The third man at the table, Feodor Vronsky, is a brilliant writer and art critic. He is also editor of the finest newspaper in St Petersburg. He is witty, very handsome, has melting brown eyes and a smile to charm the pearl out of an oyster. He has a rather slow, languid way of speaking and seems to weigh not only every word but also every syllable. When he is listening to Yascha Mounine, one is forcibly reminded of a barracuda circling its prey until the final, fatal *snap*! He too has a house in the country, and the topic under discussion is a fourth neighbour, Mihail Zonievski. Once again, Yascha Mounine is monopolising the conversation.

'Well, after all, what was he? It's all very strange.'

Alexei can no longer control himself. 'I don't see how you can criticise him, Yascha. Let us admit it, you too are only – I mean, you're a Councillor too, are you not?'

'Granted, Alexei, but I was never a *shopkeeper*!' He spits out the word.

Alexei is amused. 'My dear, Yascha, I fear you're an awful snob!'

'Let's not confuse snobbery with common sense!'

Vronsky intervenes. 'And what is wrong with being a shopkeeper, may one ask? I understand Mihail has always been scrupulously honest. It takes a great deal of character to retain one's integrity in a profession catering to so many transients.'

'It isn't a profession, it's a trade!' snaps Yascha.

With his sweetest smile, Alexei cuts in gently, 'May I remind you, Yascha, that you were once in trade?'

'That is quite beside the point, Alexei. Anyway, I was a merchant – and a very prosperous one to boot!'

'What difference does that make? What do you say, Feodor?'

'I say we have strayed too far from our original subject.'

'Can't remember what that was,' growls Mounine. 'Remind me!'

Feodor takes a sip of his Chartreuse and sits back in his chair. 'Why, Nadya Zonievska's birthday party tomorrow night.'

'It's hard to believe that little tomboy with the golden pigtails will be nineteen.'

'She has certainly improved a lot in the last year or two.' Yascha puffs on his cigar. 'For myself, I like Svetlana the best. She has such charm and vivacity!'

Alexei tries to sound casual. 'Quite apart from being her father's favourite. But that, of course, is immaterial.' Having set the bait, he looks across at Feodor. They wait for the fish to bite. It does!

'What do you mean by that?'

'Why, nothing at all, my dear fellow! What could I mean?'

Feodor says insinuatingly, 'Except that her dowry may be the largest.'

'Now, see here! Are you suggesting that I'm a fortune-hunter?'

'Heaven forbid!'

'Perish the thought!'

'I should think not, indeed!'

Feodor starts turning the knife. 'All the same, think what wedding presents she will get! Especially from those who want favours from Mihail and imagine he will grant them!'

'Ah, yes,' says Yascha, with a glint in his eye. 'The jewels, the fine clothes, the carriages, the wines–' He stops short. 'I'm sure she won't get any more than the other two.'

'Quite so, Yascha. For all his crude manners, he is a fair man. I am certain that all three girls will get an equal dowry. And it is considerable, never fear. I know this for a fact.'

Feodor grins. 'I see you have made a few subtle inquiries of your own, Alexei!'

'Well...'

'Humph! Trust the Cavalry to outmanoeuvre the Civil Service!'

'Why, thank you, Yascha, that is very gracious of you! Considering...'

'Well, you have to give the devil his due. Not that I think you're the devil, my dear chap, but – oh, you know what I mean, don't you?'

'Yes, now and then I do get a rush of blood to the head. But it is all too rare, I fear.'

'Getting back to this dowry business,' says Yascha, as if he has ever left it, 'Mihail wouldn't have all this money if that rich man had not left him his entire fortune—'

Feodor cuts in – 'Mihail saved his only child from that fire. He ran into the building and pulled the boy out just in time. It was in all the papers – including mine.'

Not being one to give credit where it's due, Yascha pouts. 'The boy died anyway.'

'Yes, but not from that fire. He died two years later from pneumonia. I think Mihail fully deserves his fortune. He risked his own life to save that of a total stranger.'

'Nadya says the money has never changed him. He is still honest and incorruptible.'

'I suspect Nadya is your favourite, Alexei.'

'As an officer and, hopefully, a gentleman, I cannot answer that, Feodor.'

'Well, I am clearly neither of those, because I will confess here and now that I find Trina to be far more attractive than her younger sisters. There, gentlemen, is a fascinating woman!'

'Well, her fascination escapes me altogether. I just don't understand her.'

'Exactly, Yascha! Neither do I! And that is what fascinates me.'

'She says precious little.'

'Ah, there is nothing so wonderful – or rare – as a woman who knows the value of silence!'

'Perhaps she is silent because she is stupid.'

'Not at all, Yascha. I know for a fact that she is highly intelligent. And as if that were not enough, well… have you ever looked into those great blue eyes? If the eyes are indeed the mirror of the soul, Trina has a beautiful soul. But she needs to meet a man who is her intellectual equal before she can be truly happy.'

'You certainly are that, Feodor. Her superior, even.'

'Why, thank you, Alexei. But I wasn't speaking of myself, you understand.'

'Since you like her so much, why haven't you told her so? The only time I've known you lost for words is when we're at the Zonievskis.'

'I trust you're not accusing me of being anti-social, Yascha?'

'Well, not quite that bad, but…'

'He does exchange the basic pleasantries. "How do you do, Trina Zonievska?"... "Lovely weather we're having, Trina Zonievska"... "Terrible weather we're having, Trina Zonievska," and so on, ad nauseam.'

'Never mind all that, Alexei. The time has not yet come for me to say more. One day, it will.'

'And then he will say, "Your garden is lovely, Trina Zonievska!" or even, "Do you like the ballet, or the opera, Trina Zonievska?"'

'Good luck to him, is all I can say – he'll need it!'

'I don't agree with you, Yascha. I think any man in love with Trina would have a very dangerous rival in Feodor Vronsky.'

'She is far too grand to cast her eyes in my direction.'

'Nonsense! Your intellectual brilliance, which is considerable, attracts a young woman like Trina – if you would only give her the chance to discover it. Besides, you have that little extra something – that *je ne sais quoi* which—'

Yascha interrupts him with, 'Don't use foreign words when you're speaking, Alexei! You're forever doing it. And you know I don't speak Spanish.'

All this time, Feodor has been sitting forward in his chair, the way people do when they happen to be the subject of the conversation. Yascha's interruption has clearly irritated him. 'You were saying, Alexei?'

'That extra little something which no woman can resist.'

'Oh?'

'Feodor, your eyes have the look of someone who has suffered and, better still, they speak of a stoic acceptance of that suffering. It is a challenge few women can resist. For it is their goal in life to bring comfort and generally to be man's inspiration. Your look of vulnerability cries out for sympathy and understanding.'

'Good heavens!'

Having understood precious little himself, Yascha feels bound to comment. 'Bravo! Well said, Alexei! Have a cigar!'

'Mmm... I must cultivate this long-suffering look,' says Feodor.

'Ah, well, the beauty of it was your unawareness of it.'

To Yascha, it seems the conversation has taken rather a boring turn. He would prefer to talk about himself, as he is the most interesting person there, is he not? They all know that!

'I still prefer Svetlana,' he announces. 'Or even Nadya will do. Anyone but Trina. She seems to be full of secrets. I want a wife, not an espionage agent. I want a woman who talks!'

'In that case, Yascha, you must never live in England. No one will speak to you there, even if they've been your next-door neighbours for eight years. Anyway, not until you've been properly introduced!'

'Ah… England!' muses the Councillor.

'Alexei, I think you're teasing Yascha. It's a good thing he's such a good sport. Aren't you, Yascha?'

'Yes, indeed! Am I? Well, I'm sure I don't know. What were we talking about, anyway?'

The others exchange glances. There seems no end to the inanities. Still, he is their neighbour and they have to humour him, since they see each other all the time.

Alexei continues the conversation about the girls by remarking that Nadya is very sweet and that Svetlana is very chic. Yascha is, for once, in agreement, adding that her clothes are from Paris and cost a great deal.

Feodor also has something to say about her. 'It's a strange thing, but anyone meeting her for the first time might think her serious. But on closer acquaintance, you realise she is rather flighty.'

Alexei intervenes here. 'Meaning she's more like Nadya?'

Feodor shakes his head sadly. 'She is exactly like Nadya, I fear.'

'She dances well.'

'So does Nadya.'

'She embroiders exquisitely.'

'So does Nadya.'

'She is forever falling in love with lieutenants.'

'So is Nadya!' Now it is Yascha's turn to join in. Feodor now comes to the point he has been trying to make all along. 'But Trina… Ah, gentlemen, she has all the accomplishments of her sisters… plus brains!'

'That's as may be, but I'd still rather have Svetlana!'

'Very big of you, Yascha,' Alexei grins. 'But what makes you so sure her father is so willing to thro— er, give her away?'

'Well, *you* always talk about Nadya as if you're the one man *she* has been waiting for!'

Feodor raises a hand in protest. 'Gentlemen, I think we are taking ourselves a trifle too seriously – and the young ladies too much for granted. Perhaps they are already spoken for. How do we know they're not?'

Yascha, the all-knowing, cuts in, 'Because their father would have thrown a huge party to celebrate. Mihail loves an excuse to show off his latest purchase. I remember that time his tailor had made him a suit of that fine English cloth and he gave a party just to show it off. It was like seeing a bear in a suit three sizes too small!'

And they say women are cats! Feodor thinks to himself.

Yascha pouts – not a pretty sight at the best of times. 'All of a sudden, I don't feel like going tomorrow.'

'You can't be serious, Yascha! Mihail told me we were to be the only guests.'

'Well, that's odd for a start. Why only us?'

'Because we are his closest neighbours. It is to be a very small affair. The really big party will be in November for Svetlana.'

'You mean my absence will be noticed?'

'Naturally!'

'And commented on?'

'Of course! 'The others glare at him. 'Yes, Yascha?'

After a long pause, 'Oh, all right, I'll go!'

Alexei rises, remarking, 'Splendid!'

He makes to go, and Feodor is glad of an excuse to end the encounter; Yascha Mounine's curiosity value has been wearing a trifle thin. As they are to meet again in a little under twenty-four hours, enough is definitely enough!

Chapter Two

Mihail Zonievski's country house is quite grand and, truth to tell, he is very proud of it. No expense has been spared in his determination to make it a worthy setting for his three attractive daughters. Svetlana is indeed his favourite, as she is the one who most resembles his wife in looks, though not in character. Mihail was happily married to a lovely woman who never gave him a moment's anxiety. When they first met, she had just left school and her sunny nature had attracted him to her immediately. He himself tended to be rather an introvert, but Katya saw good in everything – even in adversity, when she would say, 'Don't you realise, Mischa, if we didn't have bad times, how could we appreciate the good ones?'

She had worked with him in the shop and it prospered because people liked the way she treated them. She seemed always to have time to listen to their troubles and she gave them the feeling that they were the only ones she wanted to talk to. Nor was this done with any ulterior motive; her interest was genuine.

When the first baby arrived, she had a small part of the room at the back of the shop turned into a nursery. But when Svetlana came along, things were not so easy, as Trina was walking by now and could get into all sorts of mischief. She had the normal child's curiosity and Katya was terrified her daughter might run out onto the street while she was busy with a customer. Mihail understood how she felt and he engaged as an assistant a middle-aged neighbour who needed the money. So Katya was happy to stay home with the two girls, and when Nadya made her appearance, she really had her hands full.

By this time, the shop was doing well and Mihail was able to afford a small house outside the city, where the girls could play in the garden. As they grew, their mother taught them to embroider – she herself was very proficient – and also showed them how to run a home. She could not help noticing that only Trina seemed to take an interest in all she was taught; the other two were too keen on clothes for their dolls or themselves.

They were a very happy family, but later when the girls were away for most of the day, Katya went back to the shop to give a hand.

Then tragedy struck. There was a fierce blizzard which came so fast no one had time to prepare for it. Mihail had gone to deliver some provisions to an old housebound lady, and Katya was in the shop with their elderly assistant. As was customary, there were several things outside the shop on display. The assistant ran to bring them in but Katya would not hear of it. She insisted the woman stay inside and began bringing in the merchandise herself, with the result that she got soaked to the skin. By nightfall, she was very ill indeed. In those days, although one barely survived a cold, pneumonia was a foregone conclusion. Within a few days, Katya was dead.

Mihail was devastated, and he and the children were like lost souls. Katya had been their life and their sunshine. No one could ever replace her – and no one ever did.

Mihail was grateful that Trina took over the care of her sisters; at sixteen, she was very capable and mature beyond her years.

Then one evening, when he had just closed the shop and started for home in his little dray, Mihail noticed flames coming from a large house at the edge of town. He urged his horse to a trot and when he arrived, he saw several people outside but all they did was wring their hands. A lame man was trying to go into the house, but the heat turned him back, causing him to lose his balance. He kept crying, 'My son is in there! Won't anybody help me?'

As soon as Mihail came level, he jumped down from the dray and, having heard what the man was saying, he pushed him aside. 'Where is the boy?' he demanded. 'Upstairs or downstairs?'

'Downstairs!'

'You stay here! No sense in both of us getting burnt!'

As he was saying all this, Mihail wrapped a handkerchief round his nose and mouth. Running in through the flames he found the boy unconscious in a corner and swiftly brought him out.

Meanwhile, the child's father had fallen to the ground. He had made a superhuman effort to save his son, but it had not been enough. God be praised, this stranger had arrived and the child was alive! By this time, the fire brigade had come and they were setting up their hoses.

Leaving the boy with his father, Mihail made his way home. The girls screamed when they saw him: his clothes were burnt and he had no hair on his head.

By the following morning, the fire was big news in all the papers of St Petersburg and the boy's father was asking people to find out the identity of the brave stranger. Someone who had recognised Mihail told the papers, and then everybody knew!

This afforded Mihail no particular pleasure and he gave short shrift to anyone who tried to lionise him. The boy's father came to the shop to thank him, but very soon realised his mistake in proffering an envelope. As far as Mihail was concerned, he was glad to have been in the right place at the right time and that was that. The banker apologised and added that he would always remember Mihail's selflessness.

Two years later, the boy caught pneumonia and died within the week. The heartbroken father, already a widower, now lost the only loved one left to him; he did not outlive the child by many weeks. And that was how Mihail inherited an enormous fortune.

It did not change him, apart from enabling him to buy a much larger house in the country and exquisite clothes for his three daughters. The girls persuaded him to sell the shop, but for someone used to work, time lay heavy on his hands. Eventually he became a Councillor, the position he now held.

On this particular evening, the Zonievskis are preparing to celebrate Nadya's nineteenth birthday. The dining room table has been set for seven and the girls are there to see that all is as it should be. They make a pretty picture: Trina is in burgundy velvet and wears a striking piece of jewellery that sets off her classic beauty; Svetlana's elegant blue taffeta is highlighted by sapphires glowing against her milky-white complexion and Nadya is all gold colours, to match her hair. Even the robe she wears over her dress is coloured gold. In her chignon – today she is old enough to have a chignon – is a topaz brooch matching the bracelet on her wrist.

Of the three girls, Trina has the most attractive voice; there is an almost velvety texture to it. Svetlana's cracks now and then, giving one the impression that she is joking. Nadya's can only be charitably described as 'giggly'.

As usual, the two younger girls are chirping away and being no help at all. They want to change the placecards, Nadya refusing to be seated next to Mounine.

'All he ever talks about is his work in the department – as if anybody cares!'

Svetlana snaps at her to go and get ready.

'I *am* ready – I've only to take off this robe.'

'You know how angry father gets when any of us is late.'

'But I'm allowed to be late this evening. After all, it is *my* birthday!'

'Only until midnight,' Trina remarks dryly. 'At this rate it'll be dawn before you've done with the fish course! And don't look at me like that, Svetlana. You're just as bad as Nadya; neither of you has any sense of time – or courtesy. It's bad manners to keep people waiting.'

'Oh, Trina, do stop lecturing!'

'Now, girls, no squabbling on my birthday. Positively not allowed! Look, Svetlana, I'm wearing the bracelet you gave me, and Trina, see how well your brooch looks on my chignon! They are lovely presents and you're both very sweet – even if you are my sisters!'

'Thank you very much!'

With the sound of carriage wheels on the gravel path outside, there is a rustle of skirts as the two younger girls run to the window. Suddenly there is a characteristic whoop from Nadya.

'Oooh! It's Alexei Terkov! He looks simply divine! That cavalry uniform is ravishing! Trina, couldn't we—'

'No!'

'Just this once?'

'Why not?'

'Svetlana, you know perfectly well why not. We've been through all this a thousand times.'

'But we're sick of lieutenants. Besides, I like Captain Terkov.'

'And I'm sure he likes Nadya. And there's a perfectly darling major in the 14th Cavalry who would be just—'

Trina stamps her foot. 'I said *no*! Do you want people to talk about us the way they do about father?'

'But we're nothing like father!'

'We're still his daughters – nothing can change that. A captain – or a major – wants a wife he can present to the best society.'

Svetlana draws herself up. 'We're presented to the best society and they come and visit *us*.'

'But how often are we invited to visit *them*? You know how much I love father, but it's best to face the truth – that no high-ranking gentleman would tolerate a father-in-law who behaves the way father does now and again.'

'Oooh, Trina! What a dreadful thing to say! Why, if God overheard you, we'd have a catastrophe on our hands in no time!'

'Don't be so childish, Nadya! Do you really think God has nothing better to do than to eavesdrop on our chatter? I assure you, His time is better employed!'

Svetlana swishes her skirt in a gesture of annoyance. 'How I hate that Polievska creature! Imagine saying that about poor father! I'll never forgive her, that's what!'

'Neither will I!'

'And then where will she be?'

Svetlana turns on her sister. 'Never mind the sarcasm, Trina… If we tell all our friends, they won't speak to her ever again!'

'Have you taken leave of your senses? Do you intend to tell everyone what Olga Polievska said?'

'Well, we wouldn't have to tell them *exactly*.'

'Then how could they get angry enough?'

'We'll make something up.'

'You're simply proving my point, Svetlana. You are not mature enough to consider anything above a lieutenant. Now go upstairs both of you and get ready. No, not through the hall or you'll be seen.'

The two girls go out through another door, grumbling all the while. Nadya says quietly, 'No wonder all the men talk to *us* when they visit! She's always so grim!'

'I'm beginning to think she'll stay an old maid, poor thing!

Men don't fall in love with girls who are forever thinking. It isn't normal!'

'It isn't even healthy! Is it?'

Back in the dining room, Trina is trying to put things to rights, by rearranging the placecards.

She is too absorbed in the task to hear Alexei creep up behind her. He plants a kiss on the back of her neck and before she can call out, places a hand over her mouth.

'Shh! Be a good, quiet girl and I'll take my hand away.'

She nods and he does.

'Really, Alexei, why don't you think before you—'

'How can I be expected to think when I'm with you? Besides, the back of your neck was too tempting.'

'I never even heard you come in!'

'All the fun would have gone out of it, then.' He sits on a chair. 'When are you going to marry me, Trina?'

'I'm not. I've told you before... too many times.'

'And I've told you before, too. I'll marry you even if I have to wait until I'm decrepit and you're using an ear trumpet! Come to think of it, I may not live to be decrepit. I may be killed in action. How will you feel, knowing I'm lying somewhere, mortally wounded on some distant battlefield! Won't your conscience bother you?'

'Don't be absurd, Alexei! You know I don't love you when you talk like that.'

He springs up from his chair. 'Aha! So you *do* love me!'

'I didn't mean it that way.'

'You've always told me to believe what you say. You've finally convinced me! Look here, just say yes and we can stop arguing.'

'Dearest Alexei, you know very well why I can't say yes.'

'Tell me again! And again and again.'

Taking a deep breath, she begins, 'Because I am a shopkeeper's daughter and you will one day be Count Terkov and ADC to His Imperial Majesty Nicholas, Tsar of all the Russias.' Then she exhales. As Alexei claps his hands, she turns to face him. 'Why did you make me say it again?'

'For an excellent reason. I calculate the more you say it, the more absurd it will sound and you'll finally see the light. Will –

you – marry – me?'

'Do you know, Alexei, suddenly an awful thought has struck me!'

'Now what are you talking about, Trina?'

'I can't explain right this moment. It's something I have to prove to myself. I only hope I'm wrong.'

'As usual, you're speaking in riddles. I give up!'

There is the sound of another carriage arriving outside. Alexei takes no notice, but steals a grape from the table decorations. Trina raps him sharply on the fingers.

'Put that grape back where you found it! And you'll have to stop all this nonsense – someone's just arrived.'

'As I was saying before I was so rudely interrupted – will you marry me?'

Trina swallows hard and, looking him in the eye, says, 'Yes!'

Alexei is at sixes and sevens but speaks slowly.

'Did you say "yes"?'

'I did!'

'I don't believe it! It can't be!' he exclaims, and dashes out of the room.

She hears a sound, as if he has collided with someone, then the front door slams. Her shoulders sag and she thinks to herself, I was right, he only wanted me as long as I kept saying no. Oh, why do I always have to prove everything?

Hearing a sound, she turns and meets her father's puzzled look. 'Oh, Father, I didn't hear you come in.'

'What was all that about? Alexei Terkov nearly knocked me down. Rushed out of the house like a thousand devils were after him. What did you say to him to make him act like that? Another of your witticisms? Now listen here, my girl,' he wags a finger, 'too much brains ain't good for any man – makes you sick and all, but for a woman, they're death! Well, speak up! Why did he leave so suddenly? Seemed all right a while ago in the parlour. We had quite a long talk.'

'I… er… I think he said something about having to be back on duty unexpectedly.'

'Strange!' This is accompanied by a belch. 'Why did he come at all, then?'

Trina does some quick thinking. 'To bring Nadya's gift, I suppose.'

She is relieved when her father confirms that Alexei has indeed brought something for her sister. He adds, 'By the way, Yascha Mounine's just arrived. Think you could lower yourself to talk to a common Councillor?'

'You're a Councillor, Father, and I'm very proud of it.'

He looks at her then turns away as he says the next words quietly. 'Even if it is like trying to make a silk purse out of a sow's ear?'

Trina leans against a chair to steady herself. 'Oh, no, how on earth…'

'Did I hear it? Simple, my dear. Olga Polievska's voice has great carrying power – and the corridors in our building echo a good deal!'

'Oh, Father, that's monstrous!' She starts to cry. 'I'm so sorry!'

'Well, it isn't your fault, my child. Besides, it's no more than the truth. Wearing fancy clothes and decorations don't change a humble shopkeeper into a great gentleman. What I *do* resent is being accused of putting on airs.'

Trina counters with, 'And you've never done that, Father. Why is she so vicious?'

'Well, her husband came to ask me for a favour I couldn't grant, unless I wanted to end up in prison. Quite simple, you see.'

They are interrupted by the entrance of Yascha Mounine. Trina turns away to dry her tears and her father addresses Mounine.

'Ah, there you are, Yascha! If you want a drink, just ask Trina. And she probably won't give it to you!' Chuckling to himself, he leaves the room.

Yascha turns quickly to Trina and kisses her hand repeatedly. After the conversation she has just had with her father, she is totally deflated and when Yascha speaks to her, her response is toneless at best. Yascha is, of course, his usual insensitive self.

'You look well, my angel. Ah, I can always tell!'

'You look well, too, Yascha.' She speaks mechanically but he takes her words as an encouraging sign and kneels before her, this time grasping both her hands. She tries to withdraw from a somewhat absurd situation by pulling her hands away, but the terrier in Mounine now manifests itself. He is not about to let go!

'Trina, my love, before anyone comes in, you must say you will marry me!'

'Must I? Oh, Yascha, do get up! You know I can't marry you. I've told you before. Why won't you listen?'

He gets up, dusts his knees with the aid of an enormous green handkerchief, and faces her. 'You'd better give me a more satisfactory excuse than last time! I won't give up, you know!'

Groaning, she thinks hard, then says, 'My father is a widower.'

'You know very well you can't marry your own father. I mean to say, it isn't even legal, dash it!'

She is beginning to lose patience with him – far too early on in the evening. She looks round for something to do which will occupy her hands, determined to resist the temptation of emptying the contents of the gravy boat on his head.

'Really, Yascha, sometimes you are exceedingly obtuse; I have not the slightest intention of marrying my father. What I am trying to tell you is that in the next year or two my sisters are bound to get married and he will be left on his own.'

'We'll take him to live with us. Don't worry, he won't starve! I have money!'

'It isn't a question of economics, Yascha, don't you see? It's a moral issue.'

'Well,' he huffs indignantly, 'I don't see that it is at all *im*moral if he lives with us.'

She looks at him in some wonder. 'You know, Yascha, now and then I think you do it on purpose!'

'Do what, my buttercup?'

'Never mind. You wouldn't understand.'

'That's just the trouble. I don't understand you, Trina, and that doesn't make me too happy, though I know some men like it. I know that for a fact – men like Feodor Vronsky, for instance.'

At the mention of Feodor's name, she is instantly alert. 'Why, what did he say?'

'Well, he said he admired you because he didn't understand you.' He adds ingenuously, 'I had to be a good boy and pretend I didn't like you. I played my part awfully well. I remembered what you'd said about not wanting everyone... to know' (here he drops his voice) 'about *us*!'

'It's all right, Yascha. Nobody's listening. But I'm glad you didn't forget what I told you. What else did Feodor Vronsky have to say?'

'I can't think right now.' He admires his manicure and remarks casually, 'You know, when he and Alexei Terkov get together, they go on talking for ages and ages!'

She stiffens when she hears this and encourages Yascha to continue. For once, he commands all her attention. Needless to say, her reactions have gone unnoticed.

'Yes, we all had dinner at the Club last night. Of course your name came up while we were discussing tonight's party.'

'And what *about* Alexei?'

'Oh, don't worry, I fooled him, too! Ah, my little skylark, don't be afraid!'

'Let's dispense with the bird life for the moment. Do you remember what Feodor Vronsky had to say?'

'He said you are probably brilliant and he thinks he is brilliant, too, if not more so!'

'Indeed! Modest, is he not? And I always thought he had such good manners; but I see I was wrong.'

'Well, now, since you put it that way, I think I may have got it a bit muddled.' He pauses, then brightens. 'Yes, I did. It was Alexei who thought Feodor was just as brilliant as you, or even more so.'

'That sounds more feasible. And what did Feodor have to say to that?'

'Oh, something about you being too good for him or that he wasn't good enough for you – or some such nonsense.'

'Thank you very much!'

'That's all right! I thought you'd be pleased!'

The gravy boat is becoming more tempting, but now Mounine's mood changes.

'Now, see here, Trina, it seems to me that you are rather too interested in what Feodor Vronsky had to say! I mean...'

'You are quite right, Yascha. There must be more exciting topics to discuss.'

'Of course there are. Let us talk about – myself!'

Chapter Three

It will not come as a surprise to report that the party has not been a resounding success. The absence of Alexei Terkov robbed it of what would have been a happy occasion. Nadya has felt this a great deal as she fondly imagines she is his particular favourite, due to his constant teasing of her. However, an unexpected incident has occurred. As they were all enjoying their coffee in the salon, Trina had occasion to look for something in the dining room and, at her place at table she found a note addressed to her – the writing unfamiliar. But the message was all too clear:

Please meet me in the rose garden at 11. Do not fail me, beloved.

It was unsigned.

So now, at three minutes to eleven, her curiosity has got the better of her and she is in the rose garden. Inside the house, Yascha is favouring the company with the one and only joke in his repertoire.

At two minutes to eleven, Trina loses her courage and, tucking the note into the bodice of her dress, makes for the house. She has been forced to draw one conclusion: that Alexei must have left instructions to one of the servants for it to be put in place at a certain time – which meant he was coming back. It surely cannot have come from either of the men in the salon.

In her haste to leave the garden, she almost collides with Feodor Vronsky. Being rather ill at ease with him, she becomes flustered. In fact, he is as much of an enigma to her as she is to him. He checks her progress by kissing her hand.

'I'm glad you didn't fail me, beloved!'

'How dared you read that note? It was addressed to me! You had absolutely no right to do so!'

'I am delighted you didn't suspect me, otherwise you might not have come out here at all.'

'You mean *you* – it isn't possible! You of all people!'

He sighs. 'Me, of all people. Why not – am I not human, have I no feelings?'

'It's not that, but you always seemed so remote.'

'Surely you know how I feel about you?'

'I think you are making fun of me.'

He is becoming a little exasperated. 'Well, now, who did you *think* wrote that note, Trina?'

'I'm sure I don't know. I thought perhaps...'

'Not Yascha Mounine, certainly. His notion of a secret rendezvous would be the fourth bench from the right in the public park at noon! Alexei Terkov, perhaps, except that he isn't here. And I should dearly like to know why he's not. Last night he was very much looking forward to coming. Anyway, to get back to what we were saying, who else could it be, except me, of all people?'

She sits, indicating for him to follow her example, although she has chosen a seat that has room for only one person. He avails himself of a bench across from her and watches her closely, unnerving her even more. She pulls herself together.

'Come to think of it, Yascha did mention that you had discussed us at dinner last evening.'

'Yascha talks too much and says almost nothing. I am certain his report suffered in the translation!'

'No doubt! But he is not such a bad man, really. He means well.'

'Most of the calamities of this world are brought about by those who mean well – which is why they are so dangerous. I notice you stand up for him. He isn't your type, surely?'

'Is there such a thing as "my" type? Or yours, come to that?'

'The first part of that question I can only hope for; the second is simple. In a word: Trina!'

Now she really is unnerved and she rises. 'I think we had better go inside. They'll be wondering where we are. We've been here a long time...'

'You can set your mind at rest on that score. Yascha is giving a minute-by-minute account of his day in the department. It will take an hour or two before we are missed. May we not sit down again?'

It is with some reluctance that she agrees to this.

'That's better. Now, where were we?'

'We were speaking of types and you thought I was your type. That might not really be so, you know.'

'It's possible. All the same, I'm inclined to give you the benefit of the doubt.'

'Very handsome of you, Feodor. I can see you are a generous man!'

'And I can see you are a very sarcastic woman.'

'Did you expect me to be flattered by that remark?'

'I admit it did sound a trifle gauche, but it was not really meant to be high-handed. You didn't have to pounce on my words like that.'

'As a writer, I expect you to have an extensive vocabulary. You should have no difficulty in choosing the right words. Doesn't your editor ever find—'

'You forget, Trina, that *I* am the editor.' This is said very quietly, for he fears she is slipping through his fingers. He will have to tread very softly indeed if he is not to miss a golden opportunity like this. Her momentum is temporarily checked, but then she opens her mouth to fire off another salvo. Then she stops and turns to face him.

'Why are we fighting like cat and dog, Feodor? You've known us a few years and you and I have never talked alone before. The first time we do, it turns into a fireworks display!'

'I refuse to believe that we are fated to misunderstand each other. In fact, I shall continue by asking what is worrying you this evening – for most assuredly, something is…'

'You are very perceptive!'

'I may not have extensive command of the language, but I *am* perceptive.'

'And sensitive, too, I suspect. I apologise for what I said a while ago. It was uncalled for – and unkind.'

'I probably deserved it. Truce?'

'Truce.' She smiles. 'You know, I think there's a great deal of the little boy behind that austere literary exterior.'

Warming to his subject, Vronsky now starts on his catalogue.

'Ah, but I have other charms as well! I say my prayers night and morning, my teeth are my own, I'm young and fair, I've suffered. Oh, how I've suffered!' The reaction he hopes for does not materialise. Shrugging his shoulders, he soldiers on. 'I play at cards but never cheat, I'm proud of my literary achievements and I always finish the food on my plate. There!'

Trina is highly amused and also surprised at this unexpected facet of Vronsky's personality. 'You make you sound almost irresistible.'

'Almost? You mean I'm somewhat less than perfect? How can that be?'

Her laughter comes most willingly. 'Oh, Feodor, this is just wonderful! I haven't laughed like this for such a long time. I do believe our humours match. It's most refreshing.'

'Splendid! That's settled, then. When shall it be?'

She is still laughing. 'When shall what be?'

'Why, the wedding, of course. I don't think we need waste any more time, do you?'

'And who said I was in love with you?'

'Isn't everyone?'

She is clearly relieved that he is still in a jocular mood. 'I'm sorry, for a moment I thought—'

'On the contrary, I am serious. What is the good of waiting? We know, don't we? Say yes, Trina and I shall go immediately and ask your father for your hand. Oh, and before I forget, I have a small gift for you – I hope you'll like it.' (He takes a box from his pocket.) 'I got it this morning, during my tea break. It was the loveliest pendant they had. I know you often wear red, so I assumed you would like rubies. The pearl droplets are for your complexion. It's rather like those pendants used in hypnosis, is it not? You know – one, two, three…'

He swings the jewel to and fro and for a few seconds her eyes follow it. She has to admit to herself that it is in exquisite taste. She rises abruptly and confronts him with, 'You were very sure of yourself, were you not, Feodor Vronsky? Well, in that case, it gives me great pleasure to inform you that I shall never marry you as long as I live. In fact, I may never even speak to you again!' She strides towards the salon and turns at the door. 'Goodnight!'

Standing alone in the garden, Vronsky shakes his head and murmurs, 'She's gone! Oh, Trina, dearest Trina, you *will* speak to me again, I feel it in my bones. It isn't over yet – in fact, I think it's only just begun!'

Chapter Four

When Trina enters the salon, she finds it in turmoil. Everyone seems to be speaking at the same time, so of course no one is listening. But when they see her, they stop and all is quiet... far too quiet! Svetlana goes to meet her.

'Why, Trina, whatever is the matter? You look flushed!'

Nadya's contribution is more classically expressed. 'You look like all the Fates in one! What's happened?'

'It's nothing. Yascha, why don't you go with Father into the library and have a little *chat* with him?'

Mihail grunts. 'You don't ask if *I* feel like having a chat with Yascha. We can talk perfectly well in here, if only you girls will leave us in peace.'

'Yascha has been wanting to see our encyclopaedias for a very long time. Haven't you, Yascha?'

Yascha opens his eyes wide, to match his mouth. 'Have I? Why, I never even knew you had any!'

'I remember telling you all about them—'

'Let him be, Trina,' says her father. 'Besides, I don't want to go into that stuffy room with all those fancy books. Lot of show and all that money spent on them.'

'Father, when your guest expresses a wish it is your pleasure as a host to gratify it.'

'I don't remember Yascha expressing anything of the kind. What are you up to, my girl? And why are you whispering in his ear like that?'

Trina has indeed been saying something to Yascha, and to her relief, the message has finally sunk in. Brightening, Yascha now rises and stands over Mihail. 'Come to think of it, Mihail, I would like to see those books – very much indeed!'

Although his temper is worsening by the minute, Mihail tries to be amenable. 'I don't understand any of this. Oh, very well, come along, Yascha. If we don't move, we'll never have a moment's peace.'

With that, they disappear into the library. The two girls turn to Trina, Svetlana speaking first.

'Well, are you going to tell us?'

'She's being mysterious, as usual.'

'Not at all. There is no mystery. I have decided to marry Yascha Mounine, that's all.'

'When did he ask you?'

'Quite some time ago.'

'Oooh! Why didn't you say anything? You didn't trust us, is that it?'

'You would have blurted it out to everybody,' Svetlana tells Nadya, who resents the remark.

'So would you,' she snaps. 'What about that time with—'

'Never mind that now. Are you happy, Trina? Is it exciting? How does it feel, being in love?'

'I'm not in love.' She sits down heavily.

'You're not?' Svetlana is horrified. 'Oh, dearest Trina, you mustn't marry just for the sake of marrying. It's far better to stay an old maid. You won't mind it after a while. What I mean to say, it isn't the end of the world.'

'I know several old maids and they seem quite contented with their lot. I—'

'Nadya, do be quiet. You only make things worse.'

'It's all right, Svetlana. We are sisters, after all. We should not worry about what we say to each other.'

'You must make allowances, all the same. She forgets she is a year older.'

'I don't expect a twenty-four-hour miracle! Don't scold, Svetlana.'

But Svetlana answers with a sharp intake of breath. She lowers her voice. 'Trina, look! There in the corner. We never even saw him – it's Feodor Vronsky. I wonder how long he's been there? He's probably heard every word.'

'Oooh! How awful!'

'He looks as if he's enjoying it all.'

Trina tells the girls to take no notice. 'Ignore him. He thinks in a strange way. Not like us. But what's that?'

For, as she is speaking, there is no mistaking the sound of a carriage arriving outside. Before Nadya can get to the window to see who it can be, Alexei Terkov has burst into the room, flushed and out of breath. He makes straight for Trina, picks her up and whirls her round, crying, 'Trina, my love, I've got it!'

'Will you kindly put me down, Alexei. Oh, Father...'

Alerted by all the noise, Mihail has come into the room, closely followed by Yascha.

'Just a minute, Alexei Terkov! What is going on here? Stop all that spinning and put Trina down at once, do you hear? Have you gone mad or what?'

Yascha's indignation is all too clear. 'He has!'

Alexei puts Trina down and walks up to Mihail. His smile is wider than ever. 'Mihail, Trina has finally said she will marry me. The minute she said "yes" I rushed out to get the ring. I couldn't risk her changing her mind. Well, of course, all the jewellers were closed but I know a man at the other end of St Petersburg. He didn't take too kindly to opening up his shop again, but he helped me, anyway.' Turning to Trina, he shows her the ring. 'Here it is, my angel. Is it not the largest and most perfect ruby you've ever seen?'

Never before has there been such a silence, but this does not deter Alexei.

'Now, Mihail, stop looking like a thundercloud. I'll be a good son-in-law, I promise. Well, Trina, what do you think? Don't you like it?'

Trina feels herself going numb and for a few seconds she can say nothing. Then, 'It's beautiful, Alexei. And all this time I thought you'd left for good. That was what I was trying to prove – that once I'd said yes, you would lose interest. When you ran off like that, saying no, it wasn't possible, I was sure I was right. Well, what else *was* I to think?'

Alexei looks rather crestfallen – the smile is no longer in evidence. 'You had so little faith in me?'

Yascha now decides to assert himself. 'Excuse me, Alexei, but am I to understand that you have been proposing to Trina Zonievska for some time now?'

'For seven months.'

'But only yesterday at the Club you made no mention of it.'

'When a man has been turned down as often as a bedspread, he isn't likely to shout it from the rooftops. Besides, it was nobody's business but our own.'

'Is that what Trina told you?'

'We both agreed on it. And why are you so interested in this, Yascha?'

'Because for your information, Alexei, Mihail has just given his consent to *my* marriage with Trina!'

Alexei looks at her accusingly and her response is barely audible.

'I thought you were never coming back...'

Alexei now addresses himself to his rival. 'Yascha, may I ask how long *you* have been asking Trina to marry you?'

Yascha demonstrates some basic arithmetic, by counting on his fingers. 'Let me see now... September to December, Jan— no, that doesn't count... May, June, July, August – exactly eight months – I think!'

No one present has ever before seen Alexei in a bad temper and it is rather frightening. 'This is very serious, you know. So, that's the way of it!'

Trina stands between them, protesting. 'Now, please, both of you – I want no bloodshed on my account. Absolutely not! I'm sure the whole matter can be settled quite—'

Alexei interrupts in a tone not entirely lacking in sarcasm. 'Bloodshed? My dear Trina, I fear you are becoming a trifle hysterical. Yascha, my friend, I forgive you with all my heart, for you were kept waiting even longer than I.'

'That is very generous of you, Alexei.'

'Let us shake hands on it and remain friends!'

'By all means! We have something in common now. Trina, tonight you have shown me a side of you I don't much care for. But, as you see, Alexei and I are being very civilised about it all.'

Trina mutters, 'This is carrying civilisation a little too far!'

Alexei asks, 'You think so? I assure you, it can be carried even further. Nadya, my dear, would you accept this ring as an additional birthday gift – in token of our engagement?'

'Oooh, Alexei! Oooh!'

'As you so rightly say, *Oooh*! Mihail?'

Nadya's father nods. 'Anything for a quiet life!'

'Splendid!' says Alexei, who is his sunny, happy self again.

Yascha is not to be outdone. With great pomp and little circumstance he bows to Svetlana. 'My dear Svetlana, I regret I have no ring – I really wasn't prepared...'

'That's all right, Yascha. All the better. We can go out in the morning and choose one – together!'

'With pleasure. I take my tea break at 11.15. Mihail?'

Svetlana's father shrugs his shoulders in a gesture of resignation, then sits down. 'Why not?'

'Wonderful, wonderful! Have a cigar, everybody.' He glances at the girls. 'Well, not quite everybody, of course. Sorry!'

Mihail wags an angry finger at Trina. 'You see that, my girl! I've always told you a woman shouldn't have so much brains. It hasn't done you any good at all. See how easily your sisters got husbands,' and he snaps his fingers, 'just like *that*!'

'Yes,' Trina remarks, 'second-hand! And I'm sure they love being told they haven't got any brains!'

'Tsk, tsk, tsk! There you go, picking holes in vocabulary again.'

Feodor emerges from his dark corner of the room and gives all of them a shock. They have forgotten he was even there.

'That is really a most unfortunate habit of yours, Trina. On the other hand, I must admit you have gone up in my estimation as a femme fatale. You have proved an even greater mystery than I could have hoped for and I think—'

'Mystery be damned.' Mihail growls. 'Nobody'll want to marry her after this!'

'On the contrary, Mihail. If she'll have me...'

Trina stamps her foot. 'I told you I wouldn't!'

'And you told the others you would. So you see, my love, the future is beginning to look decidedly rosy!'

Without once taking his eyes off Trina, Feodor backs smoothly into the garden, swinging the pendant to and fro, just like a hypnotist.

At first Trina resists the temptation, but irresistibly she finds herself irrevocably drawn, not only to the jewel, but also to the man who has attracted her from their very first meeting.

Mrs Fitzwilliam Darcy

*I would like to thank Sue Birtwistle, producer of the BBC
adaptation of Jane Austen's* Pride and Prejudice, *which inspired
me to write 'Mrs Fitzwilliam Darcy'*

Elizabeth had now been at Pemberley two months. In that time, she had learnt a good deal about the daily running of a house of that size, thanks mostly to Mrs Reynolds, the housekeeper. Darcy was often away for most of the day, caught up in his duties to his tenants (duties he had neglected while he was busy courting Elizabeth); there was also the very considerable staff of Pemberley itself for whose welfare he was responsible. Elizabeth recalled what Mrs Reynolds had said on the subject when she had first visited the house with the Gardiners the previous summer.

'He is the best landlord and the best master that ever lived. There is not one of his tenants but what will give him a good name.' Quite so.

Mrs Reynolds had proved a real treasure. There was nothing she would not do for Elizabeth, despite something else she had said on that first visit. She had doubted that anyone could be good enough to marry her master. It had not taken her long to revise her opinion. The expression on Darcy's face whenever Elizabeth entered the room set her mind at rest on that score.

Mrs Reynolds was the soul of discretion and never discussed the 'upstairs' with the 'downstairs', but she had passed some anxious moments recently. Although she considered Bingley a true gentleman, she could never understand how Miss Bingley and Mrs Hurst could have issued from the same family tree. How fervently had she prayed that her master would not succumb to Caroline's blandishments (like some trapped animal, out of sheer exhaustion!) She need not have worried, for Darcy was clever enough to see through the scheming. Nor did he admire her attitude and her behaviour towards others. He was the least snobbish of men, as is so often the case with those born into the aristocracy – he was the grandson of an earl – and judged men on their merit. Miss Bingley was quite the opposite. She never ceased to declare how much she abhorred anyone who had been in trade and had a title been acquired later by any such person, her snide comments were not lacking. Mrs Reynolds thought she protested too much and it would have come as no surprise to *her* that the

Bingley fortune had indeed stemmed from just such a source.

The Bingleys were a respectable family from the north of England. On the death of his father, Charles had inherited property amounting to almost £100,000. The late Mr Bingley had intended to procure an estate to complement the luxurious London town house, but had died before his plan could be accomplished. Charles would have gladly pursued this scheme, but having found and rented Netherfield after just half an hour's inspection of it, he saw no need to rush into any other commitment for the time being. In the back of his mind was the notion that if he found Netherfield perfect, he might perhaps persuade the owner, a Mr Langham, to part with it. Certainly, the neighbourhood would have raised no objection; for Bingley, eager to be pleased, pleased others in his turn. His was such an open, cheerful nature that for him nothing was ugly, no one was unkind. He did tend to be impulsive and to rush in where angels feared to tread, but the extraordinary thing was that he hardly ever put a foot wrong. He made friends with an ease that Darcy found a trifle alarming and had tried to curb. Yet, although Bingley often turned to his best friend for advice, in this case it was no use. Bingley, in his own way, tried to cure Darcy of his habit of criticising all and sundry, hinting – very gently – that there were people in this world who found such observations not entirely to their liking!

Charles had five sisters, each of whom had inherited £5,000. Two portions were, for the time being, held in trust for the two youngest, Joanna and Alix who, being fifteen and sixteen years old, were still at school. In fact they were attending the same seminary where their older sisters had been educated, in London.

Margaret, at twenty-five just two years older than Charles, had married a rector, a Mr Penfold, and lived very happily in Cornwall, the county from which their mother had originated. John Penfold's parish was one of the loveliest in England, being at St Just-in-Roseland, where Henry VIII had spent his honeymoon with Anne Boleyn. From the Rectory windows one could look across the water to Falmouth. Even the graveyard was so handsomely situated that Mr Penfold frequently received requests for its 'use' by people who not only did not belong to his parish but were even settled outside Cornwall itself!

Margaret had endeared herself to the local community to such an extent that it was generally hoped the Penfolds would be there forever.

She had always got on very well with Charles and Alix, but Joanna was growing up to be far too much like Louisa and Caroline, so she held out little hope that she would develop a steady character.

With the arrival of Mr Hurst on the scene, she was glad to be settled so far away, for she found his indolent manner and arrogance insufferable. He would invariably go off to sleep when others were speaking (for of course, only *he* was interesting) with the occasional snore accompanying the general conversation, or a loud snort on his return to the land of the living. Louisa had been attracted to him because, like her, he was fond of display and was also a very graceful dancer. This resulted in endless invitations to soirées where there was a shortage of gentlemen. He had assumed she was a woman of some considerable property, judging by the elegance of her clothes and the town house, but he had not realised that she was spending more than she ought most of the time. For her part, Louisa had understood he owned not only a house in Grosvenor Street, but also an estate in Lincolnshire. By the time she discovered her mistake, there was no turning back. The marriage had already taken place. Her husband did little but play cards, eat and drink, and was so inhospitable that hardly anyone had seen the inside of his London house except his new in-laws. As for the Lincolnshire property, it was non-existent. The Penfolds wondered whether he had lost it at cards, for he liked to place a wager at his club now and then.

Margaret and her husband had, of course, come up to Hertfordshire for the wedding and had been captivated by Jane. When leaving, they issued a standing invitation to stay with them at the Rectory whenever the Bingleys felt disposed to visit Cornwall.

Like Louisa, Caroline also spent a great deal of money. Granted, she ran Bingley's houses with great efficiency, so he was disposed to overlook her extravagance. But he was often mortified by her behaviour, which was at odds with her elegant exterior.

Her manners left a lot to be desired and her remarks showed a decidedly feline bent. No one was perfect in her eyes, except perhaps for Darcy.

Caroline had determinedly set her elegant cap at that gentleman so that, when he married, her resentment was all too evident. However, she had finally decided that being away from Pemberley was an even harder penance than standing on her dignity with the mistress of the house. Accordingly, she promised herself that, should the occasion arise, she would favour the Darcys with her presence. As will presently be seen, the occasion did indeed arise, but in an unexpected fashion.

The Darcy union had proved unpopular in yet another quarter. Lady Catherine de Bourgh had made her sentiments abundantly clear in an unthinking letter to her nephew at the announcement of the approaching wedding. She had been so abusive, especially regarding Elizabeth, that he ceased all further communication. In vain did his wife urge him to effect a reconciliation, but he was adamant. She pointed out that his aunt's bitterness probably issued from his failure to marry her daughter, but he would not listen. She remembered what her aunt had said about him when informing Elizabeth of the part he had played in the Lydia-Wickham matter. She had remarked that he was not guilty of anything but obstinacy, and Elizabeth was now seeing it at first hand.

Privately, she was also a trifle concerned about her best friend, Charlotte. Mr Collins had been the unfortunate beneficiary of her ladyship's displeasure, as if the whole thing had been his fault. Although *he* could not imagine the reason why, to Lady Catherine it was all too clear that he was entirely to blame: had he persuaded Elizabeth to accept his offer of marriage, she would not now be Mrs Fitzwilliam Darcy. Since he found it impolitic to remonstrate in any way, poor Charlotte was the unwitting – and unwilling – recipient of his occasional outbursts. She tried to make allowances for his behaviour by reminding herself that for most of his life he had been kept in check by a father who could neither read nor write and who would never give him money for anything but university. Now that he had the living at Hunsford, his character was undergoing changes which Charlotte tried hard to understand. Yet she it was who offered him an escape from the present dilemma, by expressing a wish to have her first child at Lucas Lodge. Therefore, at the earliest opportunity, they set off for Hertfordshire, thus giving the dragon at Rosings Park time to cool her breath.

Shortly after their arrival, Mr Collins called upon his cousin. When the first formalities had been exchanged, he blurted out, 'I must advise you, Mr Bennet, that my esteemed patroness who, as you know, is the soul of charity and tolerance, is… well… exceedingly angry that her nephew has married cousin Elizabeth.'

Mr Bennet raised an eyebrow. 'Is that the reason for calling on me, Mr Collins? Lizzy has been married these two months. You surely did not come all this way simply to convey to me her ladyship's displeasure? I do believe—'

'No, indeed not, sir!' the other cut in. 'The truth is, my dearest Charlotte wished to be at her parents' home as her time was fast approaching. That is our reason for being here.'

'Ah, yes. I understand congratulations are in order.'

'Quite so, Mr Bennet. And I thank you. Pray do not imagine that all this was done on the spur of the moment. I do assure you, I have left my parish – and my bees – in excellent hands. You do understand, Mr Bennet…?' His voice trailed off.

'Only too well, Mr Collins, only too well! But if I may be allowed a small piece of advice? On your return, try to placate Lady Catherine as best you can. Although, if I were you, I would stand by the nephew. He has more to give – and longer to give it.'

This last remark produced a slight – a very slight – protest from Mr Collins. Mr Bennet was spared any further fatuous comment by the arrival of Maria Lucas, who appeared rather upset and excited. Mr Collins was urgently needed at the Lodge.

He left at once, neglecting to bid goodbye to Mr Bennet. He likewise ignored the rest of the family who, alerted by Maria's flustered appearance, had assembled in the hall. In his haste, he even forgot his hat.

When Elizabeth received the news of Charlotte's son, she wrote immediately to congratulate her friend, adding good wishes from Darcy and Georgiana.

All this had happened very recently. Now, in December, there was much to look forward to in the Darcy household. Colonel Fitzwilliam was to stay with them over Christmas and some of January, then return in February when the Bingleys would be coming for two weeks. However, the festivities would be taking on an especially merry aspect with the arrival of the Gardiners and their four children. It would also be the first time the Gardiners would not be spending Christmas at Longbourne. When Elizabeth had written to her aunt announcing her engagement, she had added,

> Mr Darcy sends you all the love that can be spared from me. You are all to come to Pemberley at Christmas.
> Yours, etc.

Elizabeth could scarcely allow herself to believe that all these plans were coming to pass. She was particularly happy that the Christmas visit had been Darcy's idea and had certain reasons for this. Since their wedding, she had gradually learnt to desist from saying she wished this or that. Although these ordinary remarks had not been intended as hints, their consequence was an instant fulfilment of her desires. He was the most giving of men, albeit with such discretion that she had forgotten what she had coveted until she would find it on her writing table, on her chiffonier and, on one occasion, on her pillow. She felt inadequate, to say the least, for she could never reciprocate as she would have wished.

She need not have worried. For his part, Darcy was more than content simply to enjoy her company, her lively wit and even her badinage. At first, Georgiana had become alarmed at Elizabeth's teasing of an adored brother of whom she stood a little in awe. To her astonishment, she saw that he took it all in good part and had even begun to venture a few – a very few – playful remarks of his own.

Elizabeth found much in her new life to afford her satisfaction. Her love for Darcy was reciprocated in full measure, to be sure, but she also derived great pleasure from the company of her sister-in-law. At their first meeting in the inn at Lambton, Georgiana had wistfully remarked that she would have liked to have a sister and so, indeed, she now had. Elizabeth had needed no further proof that Georgiana wanted a close relationship than the young girl's wedding present to her.

On their return from their honeymoon, Elizabeth had been conducted to the Music Room and there, near the pianoforte, was an exquisite harp. Georgiana was sure that Elizabeth would not be slow in learning to play this instrument and they would soon be enjoying duets. Georgiana was already proficient at both.

Elizabeth determined that Georgiana was never to feel that she was not a cherished part of their lives and set herself the task of ensuring that from then on, there would be no nervousness or apprehension. When she and the Gardiners had first been entertained at Pemberley, she had noticed how, in the presence of the Bingley sisters, Georgiana had seemed almost afraid to speak. When addressed, she would answer at a moment when there was the least likelihood of being heard. Looking back on the occasion, Elizabeth reflected that, as Caroline was so determined to have Darcy, intimidating his well-loved sister was hardly the way to go about it!

She was astonished at the behaviour of the two women, who had learnt very little at their private seminary, as far as Elizabeth was concerned. They paid much attention to their outward appearance and it was true they were continually invited to exclusive soirées. Their prowess at dancing and the pianoforte perhaps was the main reason they were invited, but Elizabeth could not help but wonder how their manners were tolerated by what was considered high society. She felt sorry for Charles, for it seemed to her that he was burdened not only with Caroline, but also with Louisa, who appeared to live more in his houses than her own – as if he owed her that privilege! She realised she was more fortunate than most to be spending the rest of her life with Darcy and his sister. Things could have been so much worse.

She already knew that Georgiana was fond of walking, so one day she said to her, 'I have never asked if you like riding, Georgiana. I am myself no horsewoman.'

The young girl confessed that she did not care at all for riding. The answer could not have pleased Elizabeth more.

'Now, Georgiana, I feel sure you know all the paths and byways on the estate, so you are the only one who can be my guide. I shall not enjoy them unless you are with me. I fear you will have to endure my company and answer all my questions. Shall you mind that?'

Most assuredly, Georgiana did not mind being included in Elizabeth's excursions. The compliment her sister-in-law paid in soliciting her help served to give her confidence, which had certainly been lacking in the past. Her extreme shyness had always embarrassed her and she felt free enough to confess this to Elizabeth.

'Oh, but you do not know how much I admire someone who is not aggressive. And I have always mistrusted people who *tell* me they are shy. I am certain that they are not, for a genuinely shy person does not wish everyone to know. Often they will do anything to hide the fact, and go to extremes. I am happy to say you are not like that. For myself, I find shyness one of the more attractive traits, so do not fret over it as if it were a shortcoming.'

Thanks to words like these, within a few weeks Georgiana had evinced an ease of manner which was most attractive. She would never be as fearless as Elizabeth, but at least she did not turn a bright red every time anyone outside the family addressed a remark to her.

Her first Christmas at Pemberley was all that Elizabeth could have wished. On the twenty-third of December, shortly before tea, the Darcys and Colonel Fitzwilliam were in the upper drawing room when a servant came to announce the arrival of the Gardiners' carriage. They went down at once to receive them.

As soon as the children left the coach, they made a beeline for Darcy. Bending down, he said quietly, 'Sheldon has something to show you. Will you kindly follow him?'

Turning to greet the Gardiners, he failed to notice his cousin's quizzical expression. As they all made their way upstairs, Elizabeth cast a glance at the colonel.

'He has been so looking forward to their coming! I cannot tell you how happy I am to find he has such a liking for children – and they for him, as you must have seen. Of course, it does help that my little cousins have such exquisite manners. Even the four-year-old is well behaved!'

'Darcy is full of surprises these days, all of them pleasant. I attribute these changes to you, my dear Elizabeth. He is truly the most fortunate of men.'

'And I am truly the most fortunate of women!'

By the time they reached the drawing room, the others were standing by one of the windows overlooking the driveway. Darcy made room for Elizabeth, so that she could see what was going on below.

The children were in a charming pony cart, decorated in the Portuguese manner. They were bouncing up and down in it, amid gales of laughter.

Their mother became alarmed. 'They will break that darling pony cart, jumping up and down like that!'

'Then it is their loss,' said Darcy, with a smile. 'For it now belongs to them. They may do as they please, provided they leave it here. It will be of little use to them in London.'

Mr Gardiner laughed. 'I fear that means they will forever be suggesting more visits to Pemberley!'

Darcy looked at him with that slight hint of amusement, which Elizabeth now knew so well. 'That is the general idea, Mr Gardiner!'

Poor Colonel Fitzwilliam! He seemed totally nonplussed and almost felt he must be in the wrong house!

After many protests from the Gardiners and fears that the children were being spoilt, Darcy succeeded in stemming the flow by suggesting they rest after their long journey.

'Indeed, we are not in the least bit tired,' Mrs Gardiner explained. 'We stayed overnight at Lambton to visit an old schoolfriend and her family.'

'A good excuse to leave them some Christmas presents,' added her husband.

The following half-hour was spent trying to persuade the children that the pony cart would not vanish into thin air the moment they alighted. Finally, the tempting offer of a scrumptious tea with delicious scones and strawberry jam succeeded where all else had failed.

Later, when they were alone in Elizabeth's writing room, Mrs Gardiner said to her niece, 'You know, Lizzy, I received a letter from Lydia a few – oh!' She saw an expression of annoyance cross Elizabeth's face. 'I see I have not been the only one to be so favoured!'

'Indeed not, Aunt. There have been several letters. Every time they move, which is far too often, she writes to Jane or myself. We do what we can, but we will *not* involve our husbands any further. I would be mortified if Fitzwilliam ever found out. Do you know he actually assisted George Wickham further in his profession by getting him a commission? Considering what he has endured not once but twice, because of that gentleman, I believe it shows an exceptional greatness of heart. He is truly the most generous of men, as I know all too well. It is very easy to give when the recipient is someone you care for, of course, but...'

'I quite agree, Lizzy, though I am certain he did all this for your sake.'

'Perhaps. In any event, he cannot go further. Certainly Wickham can never be received here. After all, this is Georgiana's home, too. It is no good their dropping hints all over the place and in this I shall be as adamant as my husband is about other matters. But to return to the subject of your letter, I hope,' she said, going to her writing table and extracting an envelope from a drawer, 'it was slightly less irritating than the one she wrote me soon after our wedding. I think this is the worst of a bad lot.' She handed it over to Mrs Gardiner, who began to read:

My dearest Lizzy,
I wish you joy. If you love Mr Darcy half so well as I do my dear Wickham, you must be very happy. It is a great comfort to have you so rich and, when you have nothing else to do, I hope you will think of us. I am sure Wickham would like a place at court very much, and I do not think we shall have quite enough money to live upon without some help. Any place would do, of about three or four hundred a year, but, however, do not speak to Mr Darcy about it, if you had rather not.
Yours, etc.

'As it happens, I would much rather not! I strongly suspect Wickham took a hand in the composition of that letter.'

'It is similar to mine,' said her aunt. 'And just as unthinking. Speaking of Wickham, Lizzy, I must tell you what my friends said last night at dinner. He is in no way respected at Lambton and everyone seems to know that when he left the county last year, unexpectedly (they know not the reason, although of course, *we* do) he also left a great many debts which your husband honoured.'

'This I did not know,' Elizabeth remarked. 'And when I consider how ready we all were to be taken in by him, even though no one had ever heard his name before he came to Hertfordshire. We knew nothing of his past except what he told us himself, for the only person at all acquainted with him in Meryton was Denny, who actually had only met him once or twice some time before.'

'Yet, when I met him for the first time, he spoke quite openly about having been the steward's son at Pemberley and how much he had admired the late Mr Darcy,' said her aunt.

'He also said that because of that admiration and respect for the father, he would never expose the son. Yet, as soon as the Netherfield party had left, he had no scruples in maligning Darcy. He went so far as to imply that jealousy had played a part in Darcy's behaviour to him! It is beyond belief how he duped us all. I should have been more observant. The fact that he could say all these things to a perfect stranger did not occur to me. Later, when I knew him for what he was, I realised that his phrases and his way of uttering them were always the same, as if they had been well rehearsed. I thought Darcy was clever, but Wickham...'

'You must not blame yourself, Lizzy. Tell me, did you show this letter to your father? I hear he has visited you more than once.'

'Oh, yes. He loves Pemberley and usually comes when he is least expected. He has never been an enthusiastic correspondent, as you know, Aunt. The first two times he brought Kitty with him. I suspect he did not trust her not to run off and join the Wickhams. Lydia was forever tempting her with officers and dances. But I am happy to say she has changed for the better. Several times I noticed her looking at Georgiana. I think she is beginning to realise that a young girl can have fine manners and still be very good company. My father tells me she has even been asking Mary's advice on what to read to improve her mind!'

'That is certainly not the Kitty *we* knew, is it, Lizzy? How does your father get on with Mr Darcy? I thought at one time he was rather in awe of him.'

'That is still so, but I hope that eventually, they will take pleasure in each other's company. The reserve on Fitzwilliam's part may stem from the fact that he heard my mother declare that Wickham was my father's favourite son-in-law.'

Mrs Gardiner was horrified. 'Oh, surely not, Lizzy!'

'My father often expresses opinions that are not really his own. He is rather inclined to play devil's advocate, as you know, especially if he is of a mind to provoke my mother. No doubt this was such an occasion and she took the remark seriously. Of course she is still unaware of the part that Mr Darcy played in bringing the Wickhams to the altar. My father does know. I was constrained to tell him when he had given Fitzwilliam his consent, for he believed him to be uncaring. I shall not soon forget his reaction to the disclosure, for he remarked that it would save him a great deal of trouble. That even if he offered to make good the debt, Mr Darcy would probably refuse.'

'As you say, Lizzy, your father does express opinions which are really not his own! And now, let us turn to pleasanter topics. How did you like the Lake District? You never hinted at the wedding that you were going there.'

'I did not know myself! Fitzwilliam was most secretive about the whole thing. I had no idea in which direction we were heading and he pulled down the shades of the coach – saying the light would tire me. When we arrived and he helped me down, I thought I would lose my breath altogether. My wonderful husband smiled and said, "this is where you should have been in July." I had thought Derbyshire was beautiful but with the autumn colours and the bluest of lakes, it was unbelievable. We were near Glencoyne Wood, so had the best view of Ullswater, where we stayed for the full three weeks.'

'Was your hotel agreeable?'

'We were not at a hotel at all. Fitzwilliam had been offered a beautiful house on the edge of the lake by a friend of his who was to be in Ireland for a month. We did all our excursions from there. But after two weeks, I could bear it no longer and begged my husband to have Georgiana join us. I could not endure for her not to be sharing all that beauty.'

'That must have given him the greatest pleasure – and Georgiana, too. We have been talking for quite a long time, Lizzy. I had better see whether the children are up to mischief.'

'Never! But you are right – I have been neglecting *my* duties, too.'

As they reached the door, Mrs Gardiner turned to her niece.

'Oh, Lizzy, I am so glad we are spending this Christmas with you! There is such a happy atmosphere at Pemberley.'

'For which you are in large measure responsible, Aunt. If you had not suggested visiting it that day at Lambton, I should not be here now!'

Needless to say, Christmas at Pemberley was an exceptionally happy time, with all the right gifts given and much music and laughter.

How pleasant it would be to report that at Netherfield the festivities had enjoyed equal success! Alas, they had not. The Wickhams came to stay, or rather to overstay, to such an extent that even the angelic Bingley was heard to say that perhaps a hint could be sent their way that they might leave. However, since this had been mentioned only to Jane, no decision was taken. As her father had so rightly predicted, they would always be taken advantage of on account of their complying natures.

The Bennets themselves were no less guilty in this regard. They descended on them daily and only departed when it was time for bed! All this resulted in little pleasure and scarcely any privacy for the newly-weds. The only person who gave no trouble at all was Mary, who closeted herself in the library at Netherfield for hours on end. She had solemnly informed Bingley that she would read every book he possessed from A to Z, always in alphabetical order, of course. He found her in there on Christmas Eve, for she had been missed when they were about to dine. She rose with some reluctance, but then her face brightened.

'You know, Charles, I am already halfway through the letter *B*. Can you believe it?'

'Pray do not hurry yourself, Mary. There is no necessity for it. I have today taken a decision which I hope will not displease you.

As it is Christmas, I should like you to have every single book in this library. They are not many, I know, but it would make me so happy if you would accept my gift... Mary?'

For perhaps the first time in her young life, Mary had been rendered speechless. Not a single, solitary solecism could she call to mind and her only response was a great hug for this wonderful brother-in-law.

Accordingly, the following morning, two Netherfield coaches arrived at Longbourne where this munificent gift was deposited in Jane's old room.

That was to be one of the few happy moments for Charles that Christmas. He vowed never to spend another at Netherfield and thanked heaven he had merely rented the house instead of buying it. No sooner were the festivities over than he wrote to Darcy outlining his plan to leave. He added that he would say nothing to Jane for the time being.

Once Darcy had been able to decipher his friend's letter – he himself wrote very neatly, but Charles would leave out a few words and, as Caroline had once observed, 'He blots the rest. He writes in the most careless way imaginable!' – it was clear to see that it had been written in some agitation. He answered it immediately and Charles found much to please him in the reply.

Dear Charles,

You have given us much food for thought in what you wrote. Elizabeth feels you have acted wisely in not confiding in Jane just yet since, as you yourself mentioned, she might be inclined to fret over any uncertainty. She adds that, despite an appearance of serenity, Jane has a tendency to worry and not to declare herself. Until the future is settled, let things stand as they are at present.

I now come to what may prove to be the most fortuitous part of our news. My cousin, Colonel Fitzwilliam, has been staying with us and I took the liberty of showing him your letter. I feel sure you will excuse me when you read further. The colonel bears the responsibility for several estates belonging to his brother who, to put it charitably, is an absentee landlord, spending most of the year on the continent. They have an excellent land agent, a Mr Jameson, who brings to their attention any property which might be of interest. Close to the colonel's house in Buxton he has seen just such a place and given my cousin first refusal. The heart of the matter is this: should you be interested in any way, we will be glad to look into the affair on your behalf. There is no sense in your coming all this way when it is only ten miles north of here. After all, there is always the possibility that it may prove unsuitable. I believe the colonel has decided against it, so you need not have any apprehensions on that score.

Here I will add a note of caution. I know that, like us, you share letters from the family. It is only natural, since we are so close. However, as you do not wish Jane to be apprised of our 'plot', I suggest that in the future we use some kind of code. I write freely at this moment, since she is to be away for a few days. But from now on, you will have to be careful. The inventing I leave to you!

Yours, etc.

Reading Darcy's letter, Bingley could hardly contain himself. Ten miles north of Pemberley could mean only one thing: that the house was ten miles even further from Meryton than the Darcys!

He wrote back immediately, giving them carte blanche, along with the name and address of his bankers. He trusted them implicitly to make the right choice and suggested that, should the outcome be favourable, they were to ask how Mary was enjoying her new library. If matters went badly, Mary's name was not to be mentioned.

Bingley now felt free to call upon Mr Langham, the owner of Netherfield. In any case, he was determined to leave the neighbourhood and was certain something would be found for him to buy. As it happened, Mr Langham had been receiving repeated offers for the house, the most favourable of which was from a large family wishing to occupy it on the tenth of June, when their own lease expired. He therefore accepted Bingley's decision, at the same time promising to mention nothing either to Jane or at Meryton, until Bingley found another house.

The day after they received the letter from Charles, the three Darcys set out for Buxton and matters proceeded apace. The colonel sought out his attorneys, cautioning them to be prepared later that day with documentation, should the property prove desirable. He had already ascertained that the present owners of Stourton Hall, for such was the name of the house, used the same firm of lawyers as himself. They then collected Mr Jameson and made their way to the estate in the Darcy coach.

On the way there, they were informed that the house was

ready for immediate occupancy. The owner, who had hoped to go into retirement, had been offered the embassy in Lisbon. The Foreign Office had added many inducements, which that gentleman had found hard to refuse. He had also been told to be prepared to stay for at least six years, so he and his wife had resolved to put the house on the market. The deciding factor had been the advice of the lady's physician, who had suggested a move to a milder climate.

They had now entered the grounds, which were very handsome. Mr Jameson was at his most ebullient when he informed them that they had been designed by none other than Capability Brown. Elizabeth was ready to be impressed.

'He was responsible for Blenheim, too, which I have visited. But pray, where is the house?'

She had scarcely finished the sentence when they saw it. Stourton Hall was set on a slight eminence and commanded one of the loveliest stretches of the High Peak District.

'But this is magnificent!' exclaimed the colonel.

'Nor will the inside of the house disappoint you, sir.'

As soon as they entered the hall, they could see that for once an agent had not exaggerated.

'It gives the impression of a happy place,' Elizabeth remarked. 'Clearly it has been very well looked after and is in good taste.'

Indeed, the furnishings were of the finest quality and very little would be required to make it perfect. After they had inspected every room and the gardens, Elizabeth suddenly realised that Georgiana was not of the company. It did not take her long to put two and two together and she found her looking wistfully at the Music Room, which was in the loveliest shade of blue. The furniture, though sparse, was elegant. All the same, something was missing.

'I know what you're thinking, Georgiana. That there is only a pianoforte to tell us it is a Music Room. What is your opinion?'

'Perhaps a harp and some other instrument,' ventured the other.

'Yes, most certainly a harp. Then, if we are invited – which is perhaps possible – we can play our duets!'

'Does that mean my brother has bought the house for

Charles? Oh, Elizabeth, how I wish—'

'Not so fast, young lady! But if he should, I can tell you this much: I shall expect you to decorate this room in the true Georgiana fashion. It will be your contribution to the Bingleys. I fear the task must fall on you, for you are easily the most musical among us all.'

When they had rejoined the others, Elizabeth confirmed her first impressions of Stourton Hall.

'It has almost as happy an atmosphere as Pemberley.'

'Praise indeed!'

'Elizabeth is quite right,' added the colonel, for whom Elizabeth was never wrong. 'Well, Darcy, what is your decision?'

'I suspect that if I were against the idea, I would be overruled. You can see for yourself that my wife and my sister are already decided on who or what is to go where or when. It appears I have little choice.'

The hapless Mr Jameson was finding the ways of these young people exceedingly strange. Rarely had he heard a lady express herself so freely. In his experience, the gentleman made all the comments about property and certainly did not solicit the opinion of his wife. Still, perhaps that was how today's modern couples behaved. He could scarcely permit himself the luxury of appearing shocked, since that might well cost him the sale of the house. Mrs Darcy clearly liked it, and Mr Darcy equally clearly set store by her judgement. Of course, he was only too aware of the fact that no one purchased a house of this size within an hour of seeing it. Even should a sale be agreed upon, minds could be changed several times. His experience had taught him always to be wary of enthusiasm, for it was most often those who appeared dissatisfied who turned out to be the serious purchasers. No, these people did not look too promising...

'I think we may go to Buxton now where Colonel Fitzwilliam's attorneys will be waiting for us. We are quite finished here.'

Darcy's crisp voice cut into Mr Jameson's musings. Buxton? Finished? Attorneys? Could this be really happening? To him?

The colonel's attorneys had waited in their chambers and soon the papers were signed and the deeds and keys of Stourton Hall were in Darcy's possession. It had all been accomplished rapidly and efficiently. Following an excellent dinner at the colonel's elegant home, the three Darcys returned to Pemberley, arriving just before midnight.

As they prepared to retire, Darcy said to Elizabeth, 'I hope we have not been too hasty. Buying a house for someone else is a great responsibility. I should not wish to repeat the exercise too often!'

'The risk is not so great in this case. Colonel Fitzwilliam told you that if the Bingleys do not like the place, he would be only too happy to take it off their hands. Do you think he regrets not taking it himself?'

'I think not, Elizabeth. It would have been one more property to take care of for his brother. I suspect he is beginning to tire of playing nursemaid to a man who cares nothing for his heritage and has apparently made the wrong kind of friends in Venice and Rome. He lives not wisely, but too well, I dare say.'

Before going down to breakfast the next morning, Darcy wrote to Bingley. After reminding him that they were to come to Pemberley towards the end of February, he continued:

Jane will, of course, be coming here for the first time and Elizabeth looks forward to showing her what she calls 'the glories of Pemberley'. As they have not seen each other since 'our' wedding, you may well imagine how their time will be employed! My wife and my sister join me in sending you and Jane our love,
Yours, etc.

Under his signature, Darcy had added a postscript.

I almost forgot. Elizabeth wishes to know how Mary is enjoying her new library.

One can well imagine Bingley's feelings on reading those closing words. Darcy had done it! Stourton Hall was really theirs! However, it was quite clear that they thought it should still be kept from Jane, otherwise the code would have been abandoned. Well, only a few days more and they would be in Derbyshire, with all the questions answered to his entire satisfaction. He knew

Darcy and Elizabeth well enough to believe they would have left nothing to chance.

Soon, he and Jane were on their way, laden with messages from Meryton. As Darcy had written, they had not met since 'their' wedding day, so there was much to talk about. The colonel was most anxious to see how Bingley would react to his new home, and Georgiana was particularly happy to see Jane again. These two gentle creatures had immediately found much in common since their first meeting and had corresponded regularly.

Jane brought news from Longbourne: their parents were well, Kitty was with the Gardiners in London and Mary was delighted with her new library – a swift exchange of glances here! Also, Charlotte's baby was adorable, with blond hair and green eyes. Oh, yes, and he had been christened Thomas Quintus.

Presently, Elizabeth rose. 'You have had a long journey, Jane. Shall we take a short rest and leave the gentlemen to their own devices? Georgiana, let us show Jane their apartments, shall we?'

'Well?' said Bingley, as soon as the ladies had gone.

'Well what?' Darcy countered. 'Is there something you want, Charles? A brandy, perhaps?'

'You know very well what I want, Darcy!'

'Oh, that!' He went across to a small table and took some documents from a drawer. 'The deeds. Oh, and the keys to the house.'

Bingley looked a trifle lost. The colonel spoke. 'I think it may well be time for that brandy!'

A detailed description of Stourton Hall followed, and Bingley could hardly contain himself.

'What a good brother-in-law I have, Colonel, to take all this trouble for us!'

'You are giving credit where it is not deserved. It is the colonel you should thank, not me. *He* it was who heard of the estate, *his* land agent showed it to us and *his* attorneys made certain that everything was carried out quickly and without any inconvenience.'

Bingley's remorse and abject apologies drove the colonel to raise a hand in protest.

'My dear man, you have no need to reproach yourself. How

could you have known what was going on in your absence? I do assure you, it gave me a great deal of pleasure to be of some help. Besides, you have not yet seen what you have bought. You may not wish to thank me at all! But as I told Darcy, if it is not to your liking, I shall be quite willing to take it off your hands.'

'I believe that tells you all you wish to know, Charles. Such an offer would scarcely be made if the property were not desirable. It is very handsome, I promise you.'

That evening, after they had dined, the colonel remarked casually, 'There is a property near here I should dearly like to see, as there is a possibility I might acquire it. I have a few reservations about it, though. It would be of considerable help to me if I could have the benefit of your opinion, Darcy. The agent has given me but two days to take a decision. Do you think you could spare some time? Tomorrow, perhaps?'

Elizabeth could see what the colonel was leading up to, so she said, 'I do not know about the gentlemen, but Georgiana and I had planned to take Jane over the whole property tomorrow. After all, she has never been here before. I know she also looks forward to visiting Lambton and the famous inn where I first met Georgiana. They serve an excellent luncheon and I rather thought of doing it justice!'

'It appears that gentlemen will be entirely out of place. I suggest you come with us, Charles.'

'Your husband is not too gifted in the art of gossip, Jane,' Elizabeth remarked, seeing Jane's disappointment that Bingley would not be of the party. 'We have a lot to talk about. And I dearly wish to hear how you enjoyed Christmas at Netherfield.'

'We shall take the horses and be back in time for tea,' Darcy said. 'I trust by then you will have exhausted all topics of conversation so that we may have a little of your attention on our return?'

Elizabeth laughed. 'Do not ask for the impossible, dearest. Our topics have no end. However, you may be certain that we shall be most happy to see you safely home. But, Colonel Fitzwilliam, pray do not let my husband's impetuous nature induce you to take the wrong decision!'

The following morning, after a leisurely breakfast, the two

parties went their separate ways. As they were riding, Darcy asked Bingley whether he would object to keeping the whole matter from Jane a little while longer.

'But I understood that once I had seen the property, there would be no point in withholding the news.'

'Let me explain,' said Darcy. 'Elizabeth quite rightly feels it is too late to tell Jane now. No, hear me out,' he continued, as Bingley started to speak. 'If Jane found out that we have been corresponding since January, she would be offended that she had neither been consulted nor taken into your confidence. The only way out of this dilemma is for you to surprise her with Stourton Hall on the day of her birthday.'

Bingley looked distressed. 'But that is not until the fourth of July! How will it be possible to keep it from her for so long? What about her parents and her sisters?'

Darcy dismounted, suggesting it was time to rest the horses. The others followed suit.

'Charles, do hear me out! In two days it will be March. In no time at all, you will be going up to London to join your sisters for Easter. The time will pass more quickly than you think. At the end of April, Mr and Mrs Gardiner are coming to Netherfield for two or three weeks – they told us so when they were here for Christmas. By mid-May, the Bennet family will be away: Mr and Mrs Bennet to the Wickhams in Devon, Mary and Kitty to the Gardiners. June was the difficult month and my darling wife has solved even that problem, thanks to Fitzwilliam here. And he will tell you the rest.' With that, he sat on a fallen tree trunk, his breath all but spent.

Bingley was astonished. Never before had he known Darcy to speak at such length. He looked towards the colonel, who said, 'Some friends of mine travelled to France last year and were most enthusiastic regarding a tour of the Loire Valley and the chateaux. Apparently, the whole thing is very well organised and always takes place in June – the whole of June. The last three days are spent in Paris and they return to England on the second of July. You would be leaving Hertfordshire on the thirtieth of May and spending the night in London, prior to sailing on the thirty-first. You will tell everyone that you will close Netherfield for the whole of June. Hopefully, no one will cover the three miles from Meryton so as to see what is going on. As soon as you have left, your staff will pack your possessions and, on the fourth of June, they will hand over the keys to the owner of the house. That night, they will leave, discreetly, and of course, make their way to your new house. On your return, you will come directly to Pemberley, where you have been invited for the whole of July.'

Darcy took up the thread. 'Naturally, you will only be spending one night with us. From the fourth, you will be in your own home.'

'Poor Bingley,' smiled the colonel. 'This whole business is becoming too intricate. And it has all been Elizabeth's idea.'

'I do believe my wife could have given Machiavelli a few lessons in deviousness!'

It would be superfluous to describe Bingley's feelings at the sight of his new home, given his character. He was ecstatic and each room evinced a series of enthusiasms. Words finally failing him, he sank into a comfortable chair and threw up his hands. 'How can I be so fortunate? What have I done to deserve such friends!' he exclaimed, looking in Darcy's direction.

'I'm not your friend. I'm your brother-in-law. And your senior. A little more respect, if you please!' he replied; and he smiled.

Bingley could scarcely believe his ears. Was this Darcy – being droll? Impossible! The colonel waited until his cousin was out of earshot.

'Yes, my friend, this is the new Darcy. You can surely detect Elizabeth's influence, can you not?'

As promised, the gentlemen were back at Pemberley in time for tea. When asked how their expedition had gone, the colonel owned he had been dissuaded from purchasing the house. Bingley asked the ladies about their day, but as soon as he could, he drew Elizabeth aside. Declaring himself to be the very happiest of men, he went on to say that the house had largely exceeded his expectations. 'And I promise to say nothing to Jane. I promise!'

On their return to Netherfield, Bingley found things a trifle more tolerable, knowing they would not be staying there much longer. Mr and Mrs Bennet still called on them regularly, but never stayed more than an hour or so. Either the novelty had worn off or Mr Bennet had impressed upon his wife the wisdom of curtailing their visits. Mary, of course, was delighted to have them back and proudly announced to Charles that she was already on the letter C. All in all, the time passed pleasantly and in April, having received all the necessary documentation from Darcy, Bingley was able to disclose his intention to take Jane to the Loire Valley. At first he was apprehensive, but his spirits soon revived when she confessed that she had longed to see the Loire and its chateaux. The least enthusiastic person about the tour was, not surprisingly, Mrs Bennet.

'I cannot imagine what possessed Charles to arrange such a journey! They will be gone a whole month, just to see a French river I never even heard of. Probably no bigger than a stream. You can't believe what these foreigners say. And they will be looking at castles – well, I mean to say, here in England we have the finest castles in the world – and the biggest. Then all that rich food – they'll both come back deathly sick. You mark my words, Mr Bennet. Just mark my words!'

Charles found it a great comfort to be able finally to discuss one of his plans openly. His nature did not take kindly to plots and secrets. He now set in motion the rest of what had been agreed between him and Darcy; he let it be known that, as they were to be away from the end of May to the end of June, his staff would be going up to London. The subterfuge could not be extended to his major-domo, Mr Tomkins, to whom the truth was revealed, for Bingley trusted him implicitly. He informed him that Mrs Darcy would be visiting her family at Longbourne in June, that on the second of June she would come to Netherfield and hand the keys of Stourton Hall over to Mr Tomkins. She would also be bringing precise directions, since the house was not too close to a main thoroughfare. He explained that the keys were not yet available, as the Darcys wished to make several changes in the house.

On the same day that he received the documentation from Darcy, came two other letters. The first was from Caroline, who begged to excuse herself, as she and the Hursts had received an invitation for Easter, which they felt they could not refuse. It was from a very high personage whose acquaintance they had made every effort to cultivate. Charles was only too happy to have them accept and even happier when he opened the second letter, which was from his sister Margaret. In it, she reiterated the standing invitation to Jane and himself and wondered when they would like to visit them in Cornwall. Charles and Jane were delighted to write that they would be free to come for two weeks at Easter, which was, of course, a beautiful time not only for Cornwall, but also for the church.

Everything was working in Bingley's favour. Had anything aroused suspicion in Meryton, Mrs Philips, always the first to know, would have told Mrs Bennet and there would have been an end to it.

The visit to Cornwall was all that could have been desired. Jane and Margaret became the best of friends, and Mrs Bingley was declared by one and all to be the loveliest and sweetest young lady in the whole world! And Mr Bingley, the handsomest of men.

Before they knew it, May was upon them and, when they left Netherfield on the thirtieth, Charles knew it was for the last time. He had only one regret: that they were leaving the place which had been the means of his meeting Jane. Other than that, he was glad to be going. He looked forward to their future at Stourton Hall and, before that, to the Loire Valley and its delights.

Four days later, Elizabeth arrived in Hertfordshire. Her first call was at Netherfield, where she was greeted by Mr Tomkins, who promptly had her coach moved to a safe place – away from prying eyes. He was a little nervous in case someone should recognise the Darcy crest. Elizabeth was amused at the cloak-and-dagger atmosphere pervading the whole house and decided to humour Mr Tomkins. In a whisper, she told him the chart she was holding gave explicit directions for Stourton Hall and then, with great ceremony, handed him the keys.

'Before I forget, Mr Tomkins, Mr Darcy has arranged for a great reserve of logs to be placed in a shed at the back of the Hall. He thought the weather in Derbyshire might take you a little by surprise.'

Mr Tomkins pronounced himself most grateful at such

consideration. He told Elizabeth the packing was proceeding smoothly – there was no furniture to cope with and of course, since Christmas, no books.

'Our task has not been too arduous, Madam, for the staff are very happy about the change. There is nothing they will not do for Mrs Bingley and they are delighted to be part of such a happy conspiracy. They have respected the master's secret plans and they all look forward to the fourth of July. The birthday dinner has already been organised!'

'I can see why my brother-in-law thinks so highly of you, Mr Tomkins. You leave nothing to chance.'

'It is my good fortune to have a gentleman like Mr Bingley for my master.'

'And I'm certain your arrangements for conveying the staff to Stourton Hall are finalised.'

Here he was in his element. He replied, 'Oh, indeed so, Madam. Eight of them are to leave tomorrow evening with as many packing cases as three coaches can safely hold. They will stay at an inn not twelve miles from here and send the coaches back with just their drivers. That way, we shall have four conveyances available for whatever or whoever is left here. The day after tomorrow, when I hand over the keys to the owner, we leave for the inn. From there, sixteen of the staff go to Buxton by the public stagecoach, where they will meet up with those already there.'

'Your efficiency does you credit, Mr Tomkins.'

Elizabeth took her leave and was soon at Longbourne, where she was greeted warmly by her parents. They were obviously impressed by the coach, for it was a very handsome one, but secretly Mrs Bennet could not understand why Elizabeth was not more formally attired. She had expected some extreme of fashion from a lady of her daughter's new eminence, but aside from the fact that Elizabeth's clothes were of a better cut than heretofore, there was nothing to distinguish her from other young ladies.

Having dismissed her coachman and arranged for him to return in eight days, she entered the house, where tea was already on the table, and her mother bubbling away like the kettle.

Mrs Bennet was brimming with enthusiasm and wished to talk

only of their visit to the Wickhams in Devon.

'I cannot tell you how much we enjoyed it, Lizzy! They are adapting wonderfully well to their new appointment, although I rather gathered they may soon be moving – no doubt to a better posting.' (Dear heaven, thought Elizabeth – not another move!) Her mother was still speaking. 'No doubt he is in line for an important promotion. George Wickham is very popular with his fellow officers, Lizzy, and has done very well without help from anyone! Although I daresay his brothers-in-law could have been of use to him, with all their superior connections. Still, he never complains, he is so thoroughly good-natured.'

Elizabeth realised that her mother had not been informed of Darcy's role in the Wickham-Lydia business and her youngest daughter had obviously not thought fit to enlighten her mother on that score. Elizabeth reflected that it was perhaps as well that the matter had not been divulged to Mrs Bennet, for by the time Mrs Philips had been told, it would doubtless have suffered in the translation. It might even have changed so much that eventually word would have spread that it was Darcy who had been aided by Wickham!

While her mother had been speaking, Elizabeth had looked across at her father and could see that he was anxious to give her the true picture of the visit to Devon. Accordingly, as soon as they were alone, she waited for his account.

'I rather feared the worst when they invited us down there, Lizzy. As you well know, your mother has always had a weakness for Lydia – possibly because she is the child nearest to her own character, though the less said of that the better! – so she tends to see things as she would wish them to be. Unfortunately, real life is not like that. The only officers Wickham is popular with are those of similar character and predilection, in other words, those who enjoy gambling and running up bills they can never hope to honour. His superiors do not appear to issue any invitations to their homes. They are very civil to them, it has to be said, but one feels as if they were being persuaded by someone even more superior to them. To be quite plain, Lizzy, I do not think he will receive any further promotion.'

'My mother spoke of their moving again. Surely not?'

'I have no doubt that the decision is being forced upon him by his creditors.'

'My aunt Gardiner told me he left a few of those at Lambton, and my husband honoured all his debts there. He and Lydia are both of such an unthinking nature and they assume help will always be available from one quarter or another. I regret to say, it usually is.' Here she mentioned nothing of the letters she and Jane received with sickening regularity.

'As I said, Lizzy, I was under no illusions when they invited us to Devon to stay with them. As hosts, they leave a lot to be desired. We were expected to dine them at a nearby inn every day. You can guess the rest. But enough of that! I miss my Lizzy more than I can say. My only consolation is that she seems to be very happy.'

'Oh, father, I have the best husband in the world and we are very contented with our lot. And now, what news of Mary and Kitty?'

'They will be back this evening and look forward to seeing you. You are already aware of the change in Kitty, but you will notice Mary is much improved, too. And by the bye, your dear friend Charlotte arrives tomorrow to spend a week with her parents, so you will be able to see the little boy, who is a perfect angel. He has even succeeded in taming his father somewhat. Mr Collins has cut down his epigrams in number and content!'

'A miracle, indeed!'

The few days Elizabeth spent at Longbourne merely served to increase her longing to be with Darcy as soon as possible. She found her mother's chatter particularly irritating but, to her relief, her sisters proved a sheer delight. Mary's library had wrought a most welcome change in her. She no longer made great philosophical pronouncements and appeared to have learnt the golden lesson that the more you read, the more you see how little you know. (Thank you, dear Charles!) Elizabeth now asked herself whether Mary's past unfortunate manner had originated from the fact that she was the only unattractive member of a handsome family. Had she felt that by working hard at reading and the pianoforte, she could exhibit her knowledge and her talent in such a way as to render people unaware of her looks? So many times, it was sheer showing-off, which resulted in rejection by those she most tried to please. But that was now all in the past, and the two sisters held many pleasant conversations together. Kitty was becoming a most attractive personality and did not mention either officers or dances. She had set out to improve herself and Elizabeth could detect Georgiana's influence. Her sister-in-law would have been amazed that she had been able to influence anybody and, at the risk of making her self-conscious all over again, Elizabeth resolved not to mention anything.

Her meeting with Charlotte was an exceedingly happy one and the change in her sisters was nothing to that in her friend.

Charlotte had never been considered particularly pretty, but motherhood had transformed her. Her looks had definitely improved and her natural serenity gave her a glow, which had never been there before. The baby was indeed an angel, though why he had been burdened with the names of Thomas Quintus was a mystery into which Elizabeth would not delve.

Charlotte smiled and remarked, 'There is no need to ask whether you are happy, Elizabeth. It is as clear as day. I was amused at what you wrote about Colonel Fitzwilliam's frequent visits to Pemberley. Perhaps you were not aware that when he was staying at Rosings and he first met you, he often came to the Parsonage on the off-chance of seeing you there. He was very taken with you, Lizzy and, to own the truth, I had rather hoped to play matchmaker. You must not blame me for such a scheme. You may remember that you often spoke of your abhorrence for Mr Darcy.'

'Indeed, I had no idea that I had caught the colonel's fancy. He is forever telling my husband that I can do no wrong, but I put it down to his wishing to tease him. And did you know that Mr Darcy first proposed to me at the Parsonage? I said nothing at the time, because I was too angry at his way of expressing himself. Oh, my dear Charlotte, how I wish everyone could be as happy as Jane and I are with our husbands!'

Charlotte could see what her friend was implying and tried to set her mind at rest. 'I am not unhappy, Lizzy, truly. With the birth of our son, my husband has so changed for the better you would scarce recognise him. He had a very miserable childhood, you know, and then when he went to university, he was spurned by the other students and accused of being miserly. So he was never one to have a circle of friends. The truth was, his father had given him nothing except what would cover his tuition, board and lodging. Not a penny more.'

Elizabeth left Longbourne with a host of different impressions; with the exception of her parents, everyone had changed – and for the better. She thought the Collinses had perhaps a chance of some domestic happiness after all, from what Charlotte had said, and her sisters certainly gave no cause for alarm. She wondered what her mother would do when Jane and Charles did not return to Netherfield as she expected them to. She had prepared all sorts of herbal remedies to cure whatever French food had done to them while they were away.

All the way back to Pemberley, pictures and phrases kept recurring. She could not help but compare her marriage with that of her parents. Mr Bennet had been attracted by Fanny Gardiner's beauty and lively spirit. Unfortunately, quite early on he had realised that she was also frivolous, unthinking and unintelligent. His affection gradually waned until in the end it was non-existent. He held his wife up to the ridicule of her children, which appalled Elizabeth. As a *husband*, he left much to be desired and she questioned whether she would have been so tolerant of his shortcomings as a *father* had she not been his favourite. She also wondered whether he and Darcy would ever become as close as her husband was with Mr Gardiner. In her heart of hearts, she rather doubted it.

There were, however, no such doubts where her mother was concerned. Her comportment in public was embarrassing, to be sure, but she recalled the expression of disbelief on Darcy's face when Mrs Bennet had exclaimed, 'Imagine, Mr Darcy, how mortified I was to learn that Lydia had no new clothes for her wedding. The disgrace of it!'

Darcy had waited for the disgrace to extend to Lydia's having lived a fortnight with Wickham, but no such pronouncement came. She also remembered her father's indifference to the fact that a total stranger should have rescued his youngest daughter from the scorn and derision of their general acquaintance. It was almost as if he considered that it had been Darcy's *duty* to help. From this contemplation it was only natural that she should recall what her mother had said when Jane informed her that their uncle was to offer financial aid to Wickham so that he would wed Lydia.

'Well, it is all very right. Who *should* do it but her own uncle? If he had not had a family of his own, I and my children must have had all his money, you know. And it is the first time we have ever had anything from him except a few presents.'

Elizabeth shuddered at the memory of those words, spoken by Mrs Bennet about her own brother, her superior in every way. The Gardiners had always spent Christmas at Longbourne, invariably arriving with a great many presents, including some for all the staff. That her mother should in any way resent them and their children was reprehensible. Her little cousins gave nothing but pleasure wherever they went and their manners were vastly superior to those of most of the Bennets. Perhaps her mother's resentment stemmed from envy, for Mr and Mrs Gardiner clearly loved and respected each other and presented the kind of united family which Mrs Bennet had not been able to accomplish in her own. She was happy that the Gardiners' Christmas visit had proved such a success, for they were to come again this year too. Darcy's affection for them was genuine and his attachment to their children had been a revelation to Elizabeth.

She had much to impart at Pemberley and could see Georgiana's pleasure when told Kitty had asked after her.

'I could scarcely credit the improvement in both my sisters. Kitty and Lydia used to quarrel and shout at each other incessantly. In a whole week, Mary and Kitty did not raise their voices once. Mary is full of praise for Charles and, I am glad to report, she has even taken to playing music of a much happier nature. Kitty has quite neglected her needlework and reads as much as she can. As for Charlotte, you would hardly recognise her. Motherhood has given her such a lovely glow and it is all due to the baby. He is absolutely angelic, gurgles happily and gives her no trouble at all.'

'I wonder you came back so soon,' Darcy remarked. 'You have been missing your family more than you realised.'

'You and Georgiana are my family, dearest. And I could ask for none better.'

Two letters awaited Elizabeth on her return, both from Jane. The first described the departure from London and the boat trip, where everyone had been ill, with the exception of the captain and crew. The second letter was a little more interesting.

My dearest Lizzy,

You cannot imagine how wonderful is this tour! The river is quite a considerable size (Mama will doubtless be disappointed!) to judge by the charts we have been given to study. But what is really magical is the situation of some of these chateaux. We have seen Saumur, a truly fairy tale castle and then Chinon, where our own Henry II spent a Christmas or two. They tell us he released his wife from her prison so that she could join him and their three sons for the festivities. Since she was none other than the tempestuous Eleanor of Aquitaine, you may well imagine how the stories are embellished over here. They tell us the occasion was a rare one, for it is not often that three kings of England are to be found at the same gathering. It was truly a family affair, for Eleanor's stepson, the king of France, his sister and her other son, Geoffrey, were also present.

Of course here Chinon is more famous as the place where Joan of Arc performed her first miracle. I am making a great many notes, Lizzy, which amuses Charles, but I do not want to forget any of this. Although it is all most enjoyable, I do have two great regrets: that, like my sisters, I cannot draw. How I should have liked to keep a pictorial record of all we are seeing! My other, even greater regret, is that my dearest Darcys are not here to share in all this beauty.

I shall continue tomorrow, as we are being summoned to the dinner table. (A further disappointment for Mama: the food to date has been delicious!)

Here the letter-writer had paused and, when she had resumed, it was clearly the following morning, since there was fresh energy in the writing and a deal more optimism.

My dearest Lizzy,

I have good news! You may recall that my inability to draw was causing me much concern. All the while our guides were showing us these magnificent places, we had noticed a young man sketching. Last evening at dinner, he was sitting across the table and I suggested to Charles that we – or rather, he – might approach him to see if he would show us these sketches. He very kindly brought us all he has done until now and oh, Lizzy, they are exquisite! One relives the experience entirely. You will like them very much indeed, I know, for the other good news is that his father's house is but five miles north of Pemberley and he has invited all five of us to visit them so that you can share what we have been seeing. He will be there all summer and the place is Denton Lodge, so possibly Mr Darcy – I mean Fitzwilliam, knows of it. He is the pleasantest of young men, exceedingly handsome, though not vain, with manners that leave nothing to be desired. In character he seems the twin of my darling Charles, just as open and sweet tempered. They are getting on extremely well and have discovered mutual friends in London, where he is a lawyer... I shall write again tomorrow, after we have visited Chenonceau...

When she had finished reading the letter, Elizabeth laughed. 'Dearest Jane, she tells us everything about this paragon, but forgets to mention his name!'

'I know who she means,' Darcy remarked. 'It is young Julian Winslow and I have heard much good about him. A friend of mine had recourse to his services and found him extremely honest. I'm sure we should all like to see his sketches if they are as fine as Jane says. It is fortunate that he is halfway between here and Stourton.'

There were two more letters from Jane, each brimming with happiness. It appeared that, apart from mutual friends, the young men had found mutual interests. For her part, Jane was delighted to be taken care of by two such amiable and handsome gentlemen. It appeared that they were the youngest of the party, so were finding each other's company most agreeable.

'Reading between the lines, I would judge that Master Winslow has aroused Jane's maternal instincts,' said Elizabeth.

In no time at all, the end of June was upon them and the three Darcys made their way to Stourton Hall for one last look before the arrival of the Bingleys. They were greeted by the major-domo and all the staff they had known at Netherfield. Georgiana took Elizabeth by the hand and led her to the Music Room. She had left certain instructions with Mr Tomkins and he had carried them out to perfection.

'No wonder you did not want me to see it until it was completed,' Elizabeth said. 'It is exquisite, Georgiana. I knew you would do the Bingleys proud.' Darcy having joined them at that moment, she took his arm. 'You can see that your sister has other talents beside music. Have you ever seen such a pretty room?'

Darcy was taken by surprise, for the furnishings matched the walls and on one side of the room where there were no instruments, was a magnificent tapestry depicting the gods on Olympus, each playing a different instrument. Unusually, the background of the tapestry was also the same shade of blue as the furniture. The pianoforte and the harp were particularly fine and there was a music stand on which rested a handsome flute.

'Indeed I have not seen such a pretty room. How clever you were to find all the right colours, Georgiana. I am really very proud of you.'

Everything else being entirely in order, they returned to Pemberley where, late on the evening of the third of July, the Bingleys arrived. After they had dined and talked almost into the small hours, Elizabeth noticed that Jane seemed a little unhappy. She asked her the reason and Jane explained.

'Well, I had so wanted to go to Netherfield on our way here to bring some more clothes. They had cautioned us to take as little as possible since we were to travel by coach. I really do not have enough with me for a month-long visit.'

'You are among family here, Jane. If it would make you feel more comfortable, Georgiana and I will not change more often than you do. There! What could be fairer than that?'

'Well,' said Darcy, 'I regret I must raise an objection. But only where the fourth of July is concerned, you understand.'

Bingley's mind leapt from birthday to gifts and he suddenly remembered they had done some shopping in Paris. The yards of French silks in pink and blue and white and the Alençon lace were much admired and Charles presented Darcy with a superb writing set from a famous Paris emporium. Jane remarked that Charles had bought one exactly like it for himself. In fact, having bought it for the colonel, he had been obliged to tell Jane an untruth.

At breakfast the following morning, Jane received everyone's wishes and her gifts. Perhaps the most charming of these, and the most surprising, was a sketch by Julian Winslow. Charles had asked him to draw Jane as she caught her first glimpse of Paris, and the picture was enchanting. However, the artist had insisted that it be his gift to the lovely Mrs Bingley.

Jane had been so moved by all this attention that the tears had come welling up in her eyes. With Julian's gift and the knowledge that it had been her husband's idea, there was now no controlling the sobs.

Darcy rose and solemnly addressed the company. 'And now, if Mrs Bingley will favour us with a dry eye… (more tears from Mrs Bingley, through smiles of joy)… I repeat, with a dry eye, we have another little surprise in store.'

'Another one?' Jane's voice was barely audible.

'Yes. You will not be staying here tonight. We have lately discovered a perfectly charming inn and we have reserved a table for dinner and rooms for the night. They keep an exceptionally fine table and I think you and Charles will have as satisfactory a meal as any you may have enjoyed in France. It is all settled and I will brook no denial from Mr and Mrs Bingley. Besides, we must not disappoint Georgiana. She has been so looking forward to it.'

Quite naturally, the Bingleys raised no objections and later on, they all set off at a leisurely pace, the ladies in the carriage and the gentlemen on horseback. Darcy had meanwhile arranged for the rest of the Bingleys' luggage to be sent to Stourton Hall an hour after the party departed.

There was, of course, no inn to go to and the Darcys would in fact be staying the night at the colonel's house.

They drove straight to Stourton Hall, where the gentlemen dismounted and waited for the ladies. As Charles opened the door of the carriage and handed them down, he remarked casually, 'Darcy has asked Colonel Fitzwilliam to join us as he particularly expressed a wish to be a part of the festivities, so we are collecting him. We are rather early, so Darcy thinks we should wait inside.'

Here he was on safe ground, since he knew that Jane had never seen the colonel's house. The only danger was Georgiana, who could barely control her excitement.

At the main door, Darcy made a great show of tapping it with his cane when suddenly it opened wide. Swiftly, he stepped aside to allow the Bingleys to go first. Mr Tomkins stood at the entrance, very erect and behind him, in a long line, were all the Netherfield staff.

'Welcome to your new home, my darling,' smiled Bingley. Darcy only just succeeded in catching Jane as she fainted. Someone quickly fetched a glass of water and Elizabeth administered some smelling salts. Aside to Georgiana she whispered, 'I thought these might come in useful!'

After a while, the new mistress of Stourton Hall opened her eyes.

'I suppose we should have prepared you in some way, but Bingley did so want to surprise you,' Darcy said. 'Not shock you, of course!'

Once calm had been restored and the conspiracy of silence explained, Jane was asked what she thought of her new home, which she had now seen, room by room.

'I think it is the most beautiful house I have ever seen – after Pemberley. Although even there you do not have such an enchanting Music Room as the one here. I insist that you visit us often, Georgiana. Charles and I do not play any instrument and I should be very sorry if the ones here were to suffer through too little use.' Looking at Elizabeth, she added, 'And you may bring your friend, if you wish, Georgiana.'

They were joined at that very special dinner by the colonel, whose complicity was finally explained, and most gratefully acknowledged. The luggage coach having arrived, Charles was able to present him with his gift – the other writing set. Jane, seeing that one more thing had been kept from her, now wondered whether she had been the only one in the dark and whether anything else was to be revealed.

'That is all!' Bingley reassured her. 'As for being kept in the dark, the only ones who knew were the staff, the owner of Netherfield, the colonel's land agent and his attorneys – and the five of us, of course.'

'It all comes down to this,' said Darcy. 'You have been in the clutches of some rather convincing liars. Even my young sister was persuaded to lie!'

'Oh, I really didn't mind,' said Georgiana brightly. 'In fact I rather enjoyed it!'

'There, you see! Totally corrupt! But then, I am in no position to criticise, since I did the same.'

'For the best of all possible motives, Darcy,' Bingley added, defending his friend.

'As for you!' Darcy regarded him coolly. 'You were the worst of the lot, keeping it from your own wife – whom you profess to love.'

'Come, Fitzwilliam,' laughed Elizabeth. 'We can none of us afford to cast the first stone, I think.'

The evening passed very pleasantly and soon, after repeated thank yous and goodbyes, the Darcys left with the colonel to spend the night at his home. But before leaving, Darcy told Charles that he would be writing to Denton Lodge to invite the Winslows to dinner at Pemberley the following Sunday. He hoped the Bingleys would be free.

'We shall look forward to it, Darcy. And you will see that Jane in no way exaggerated as regards the sketches. You saw an example this morning.'

When Darcy wrote to Denton Lodge, he hoped the two gentlemen would honour them with their presence, adding that the sketches were included in the invitation.

Accordingly, the following Sunday, the Winslows arrived, closely followed by the Bingleys. Jane declared herself to be the happiest woman in the world and, on seeing Julian, she thanked him for his gift.

'I wish it did more justice to the original, don't you, father?' Julian commented.

The remark was genuinely meant; there was little hypocrisy in the young man's make-up. As the evening wore on, Elizabeth marvelled that there could be two Bingleys in this world.

Finally, it was time to see the sketches and they were indeed everything that Jane had said. Darcy was impressed, and said to Julian's father, that one could relive the experience by looking at them from time to time.

Julian's father, a judge, was as delightful as his son, though gifted with a wryer sense of humour. Elizabeth thought that in court, he would probably be rather daunting, since he seldom smiled.

When the two gentlemen rose to take their leave, Julian turned to Georgiana.

'I gather from Mrs Bingley that you play duets with your sister-in-law, Miss Darcy. We hope you will give us the pleasure of hearing you at Denton Lodge when you come next week. We have both a pianoforte and a harp.'

Georgiana coloured and turned to Elizabeth, who smiled in encouragement, before replying, 'I'm sure we shall do our very best. Shall we not, Georgiana?'

But the young girl's courage had entirely failed her for the moment. Bingley quickly saved the situation.

'Shall we not go together part of the way, Winslow? It will make the journey seem shorter.'

When their guests had left, Elizabeth realised that Georgiana was nowhere to be seen. Eventually, she found her in the Music Room, sobbing. When asked what was the matter, Georgiana said, 'Oh, what must he think of me? I could not speak at all, Elizabeth. I was as tongue-tied as I used to be before.' And the sobbing was renewed.

'What nonsense is this? No reply was called for. In fact, had you said anything, I rather think he would have taken you for a chatterbox, and that would never do. No, you were quite right to say nothing.'

The sobbing ceased and all was again right in Georgiana's world. When Darcy finally ran them to earth, he found them searching through sheets of music.

'I thought you had gone for one of your long walks, when I did not see you...'

'We are looking for some music for next week. What did you think of our guests, dearest? Did you like them?'

'It would be difficult not to like them and I look forward to seeing them again. I should like to get to know them better.'

It did not require a genius to understand the real meaning behind Darcy's remark. Neither he nor Elizabeth could have failed to notice that young Winslow had experienced some difficulty in tearing his eyes away from Georgiana. But ever since the awful episode with Wickham, Darcy had been doubly alert in his wish to protect his sister. Soon she would be seventeen and no doubt many young hopefuls would be beating a path to their door. His only consolation lay in the fact that he was not entirely alone in his efforts to avert any unpleasantness. He knew his wife was generally an astute judge of character now, thanks to her mistaken reading of Wickham and himself in the past. The lesson had been well learnt.

During the next few weeks, the Winslows were frequent guests not only at Pemberley but also at Stourton Hall. They were equally frequent hosts, affording Darcy to make a more accurate assessment of the situation. For there was, indeed, a situation.

It was quite clear to everyone that Julian Winslow was hopelessly in love with Georgiana, although his father was discretion itself and never brought up the subject.

One day Darcy said to Elizabeth, 'I feel sure he will ask for her hand. I am responsible for her. What am I to do? If I say no, I could be robbing her of a chance of happiness and a settled life with a young man of steady character. I do like him, Elizabeth. The question is, do I like him well enough to entrust him with my sister's future? One cannot be too careful.'

'There is one way for you to be more certain. After all, you are not her sole guardian, are you?'

Darcy brightened. 'Of course! You are absolutely right – as Fitzwilliam never ceases to remind me. Let us have him to stay for a week or two. He should be back by now. And it will help that he has never met Winslow before this.'

Darcy wrote to his cousin forthwith, stressing his apprehensions. Much to his surprise, the colonel was better informed than he could have imagined. The friends with whom he had been staying had been most informative, when he had mentioned Winslow's name. His letter continued:

…here I should like to impress upon you that I was not prying, nor asking questions. The information was entirely unsolicited and came about in a perfectly natural way. I was asked how my friends had enjoyed the Loire Valley, for my hosts were the ones who had recommended the tour. I replied that the Bingleys had been most enthusiastic and had struck up a friendship with Julian Winslow, which they intended to maintain on their return to England. That was all my contribution to the conversation. They furnished the information. Most fortuitous, really. But to return to the heart of the matter. I know there has always been a certain amount of anxiety on your part that Georgiana's fortune may influence the actions and intentions

of various suitors. And rightly so. But here let me set your mind at rest on that score.

It appears that young Winslow stands to inherit not only his father but also his uncle, who has no children of his own. In addition, there is a sizeable mansion and a plantation consisting of several thousand acres, in Virginia. He has recently left his barristers' chambers in London and decided to relocate to Buxton, where his family has enough connections to ensure him work. There appears to be some anxiety about the judge's health and the young man has found it more practical to be here permanently, instead of going back and forth each time the necessity arises.

Darcy looked up at Elizabeth, to whom he had been reading the colonel's letter.

'That gesture alone speaks volumes,' she said. 'Do go on.'

'The letter is almost finished. I have never before known my cousin to write at such length, but all of it is interesting – and pertinent.' Darcy read on,

So, all in all, Darcy, the future is not too grim for master Winslow. If he does love Georgiana – and who can blame him – it is certainly not for her money. I look forward to seeing you all the day after tomorrow.
Yours, etc.

After the colonel's arrival, Elizabeth remarked, 'It is all coming together, like pieces of a puzzle. One coincidence after another. Is it fate, do you think, Colonel?'

'Just one moment,' Darcy admonished, 'before we go off into flights of fancy. We seem to be taking it for granted that Winslow will be asking for Georgiana's hand. It is quite possible that she may harbour some sentiment for him, but he himself has mentioned nothing.'

'Dearest, you have only to see them together to know!'

'All the same, Elizabeth, I think you might try and sound her out. Perhaps he has said something to make her believe that some sort of declaration is imminent.'

Elizabeth undertook her delicate mission with efficiency and tact. Presently, she was able to inform her husband of the results.

'Oh, dearest, we are back in the age of chivalry! He has never made any advances, nor has he dropped any hints. There is no question of his "toying with her affections", as they say. In fact, she is thoroughly convinced that her love is not reciprocated. No one can accuse him of leading her astray. She is completely unaware that he "worships her from afar". Can you believe that?'

'It has been known to happen, Elizabeth.'

'Not possible! A woman always knows – instinctively.'

Darcy looked at her and said quietly, '*You* did not!'

To that, there could be no riposte. She sat silent, listening to a plaintive melody coming from the Music Room, where Georgiana was at her pianoforte.

Darcy started pacing round the room, as he had done before his proposal at the Parsonage. She knew the signs well enough to see he was really agitated.

'What is to be done, Elizabeth? I can hardly confront him as regards his intentions when none have been declared.'

'What does your cousin think? Ah, here he is!'

As the colonel entered the room he asked, 'What do I think about what, Elizabeth?'

'We were speaking of Julian Winslow and Georgiana. What is your opinion? I think there is mutual affection there. I also think that there is reserve and timidity – on both sides.'

'Ah, well, that is no concern of mine!' And with that, he sat down.

Darcy and Elizabeth stared at him. It had been a rather callous remark, given the colonel's normally gentle nature. Before they could say anything, a servant entered and addressed himself to Darcy.

'I beg your pardon, sir, but Mr Winslow wondered whether he might have a word with you?'

'Of course, Blake. I shall be in my study.' As the servant left the room, Darcy turned to his cousin. 'Anything I should know before I see him?'

'Nothing in particular,' the other shrugged. 'Anyway, it may not be what you think. I would not read too much into this, if I were you.'

After Darcy had left, Elizabeth turned to the colonel. 'Do you think…?'

'No, I don't think. I know!'

'But how?'

'Well, young Winslow approached me as I was strolling in the grounds just now. After much coughing and clearing of throat, he owned that he was very much in love with Georgiana. He then said, rather wistfully I thought, that Darcy would probably never countenance such a match. I suggested he put it to him, just the same. One never knew, I said. One might always be in for a pleasant surprise, I added. Then he wondered whether Georgiana felt anything for *him*. She had never shown any especial partiality, he thought. I explained that her natural modesty would preclude any demonstrations of the kind. Oh, dear, it was such an uphill struggle, Elizabeth. Finally, I clapped him on the back and told him that if she was not worth the effort, he had better abandon the whole matter. At that, he shot off like a rabbit.'

'In which direction?'

'Oh, dear, I do hope I did not make things worse. What have I done, Elizabeth?'

'No harm at all, I am certain,' she replied, in an effort to placate him. However, she herself had her doubts.

'He is an exceptionally nice young man and has his wits about him as a general rule.'

'Indeed. And he appears to have many good qualities.'

'Quite so. Qualities which recommend him to all three Darcys: loyalty, honesty and strength of character, which my husband always looks for in others; an affectionate nature and great natural courtesy, so Georgiana is taken care of; and a quick wit and sunny temperament, ensuring appreciation from me.'

At that very moment, Darcy entered the room, looking rather solemn. The hapless colonel feared the worst. Darcy shrugged his shoulders and sat down heavily. As the others started to speak, he raised a hand in warning and gave the impression that he was listening for something in particular.

Suddenly, the plaintive music they had been hearing turned into a cacophony of sound, as if someone had been abruptly interrupted.

'There!' said Darcy. 'No need for words, you see!'

Later, when the inevitable hugs and congratulations had been exchanged, Georgiana took her sister-in-law aside, declaring she was the happiest creature in the whole wide world.

'He loves me, Elizabeth! He has always loved me! Can you believe it!'

'Jane spoke those very words when Charles proposed. And I imagine I was no different when I became engaged to your brother. But I think we should send an express to the Bingleys, since they were responsible for your meeting Julian in the first place.'

The reply from Stourton Hall was by the very same messenger. Charles insisted on being groomsman and wrote that both he and Jane were absolutely delighted at the news of the betrothal.

The following day, as Elizabeth was writing to her aunt, Georgiana put forward an idea, which was positively inspired. Would the Gardiners please allow their children to be her wedding attendants?

The acceptance was not long in coming.

My dear Lizzy,

It will come as no surprise to you that the children (and their parents!) are delighted with Georgiana's suggestion. However, at the risk of sounding ungracious, I must add my hope that it will not be a very long engagement as the children are growing out of their clothes at an alarming speed!

Yours, etc.

Elizabeth wrote back to reassure her aunt as to the length of the engagement.

In point of fact, the date of the wedding has now been moved forward. Judge Winslow has become quite ill and his condition is giving ever greater cause for alarm.

You will remember that Jane brought some beautiful silks from France and work has already started on Georgiana's bridal gown and her travelling ensemble. In order to save time, a seamstress leaves here tomorrow with more of these silks – in blue and pink – for my little cousins. She has strict instructions to follow all your advice as Georgiana puts great store by your good taste. You will find Mrs Sheldon ready and willing and, of course, most trustworthy. You may remember it is her husband who takes care of the children's pony cart!

Yours, etc.

As Elizabeth had mentioned to her aunt, there was a great deal of anxiety at the Winslow home. Julian's uncle and his wife had come to Denton Lodge and everyone prayed that no tragedy would mar what all hoped would be a happy occasion.

However, the apprehension was not all one-sided. Georgiana confided to Elizabeth that she felt uncomfortable that they could not make some gesture towards Lady Catherine.

'I would have written to her myself, but I did not think it was right for me to do so, even though she is my aunt,' she told her sister-in-law.

'You used good judgement there, my dear. I have tried several times to persuade your brother, but I meet with refusal. Perhaps if *you* were to say something, he might listen. For my part, I have tried everything.'

It may have been the fact that up till now, Georgiana had not even mentioned the name of her aunt for fear of angering or even offending Darcy. He had always said he would do anything for his sister and when she appealed to him so plaintively, he suddenly relented. Accordingly, an invitation went out to Rosings Park for Lady Catherine (and Miss Anne de Bourgh).

This was received with some surprise by his aunt. At first she considered declining, but she thought better of it. To own the truth, polluted woods or no, she was burning with curiosity to see whether Elizabeth had made any changes at Pemberley, for, as she herself had often remarked, she was exceedingly attentive to such things. She was determined to be displeased, but she accepted the invitation, nevertheless. As Mr Collins could not for the moment find anyone to replace him at the Parsonage, Charlotte was to travel up to Derbyshire with the two ladies, leaving her son with her parents for a few days. Elizabeth reflected that her friend's placid nature would compensate for the abrasive behaviour which Lady Catherine was sure to bring with her from Rosings. It was therefore with some surprise that Elizabeth saw that Lady Catherine was now on her best behaviour and even deigned to be pleased with all she saw. Elizabeth reflected that she was perhaps fearful of being once again estranged from her nephew, who, she would have to admit, was a supremely happy man. That, at least, was what Elizabeth told herself.

When the bride entered the church on her brother's arm, the congregation fell silent. In her magnificent bridal gown, Georgiana was a vision of loveliness and the four children attending her were declared to be little angels. Darcy, concentrating hard to avoid treading on all those yards of silk, did not look up until Georgiana stopped and he realised they were near the altar. He then stepped back and joined his wife in the front pew.

The ceremony was perfection. Now and again, Elizabeth cast an anxious glance at the groom's side of the church and saw Julian's father standing very erect, his brother and his sister-in-law on either side of him. It was clear that Judge Winslow was making a superhuman effort for the sake of his son. Elizabeth prayed fervently that nothing untoward would happen that day – and nothing did.

As Georgiana started to walk down the aisle on her husband's arm, she smiled warmly at her father-in-law and then, stopping suddenly in front of her brother, she kissed him and then continued to the door of the church.

Elizabeth was happy that the young bride had made such a handsome gesture and she could see how much it had moved Darcy. 'Well,' she thought. 'We are still a family. Plus one!'

As may be imagined, the wedding reception at Pemberley was a very splendid occasion. Darcy's first thought on arriving was to make sure that Julian's father was comfortably settled. He also cautioned Mrs Reynolds to be at all times conscious of the place where the physician could be found – just in case. Then he resumed his duties as a host, first complimenting the Gardiner children who had, as usual, behaved like the little angels they were.

Caroline Bingley had finally found an excuse to visit Pemberley again. Ever since she had lost Darcy to 'that coarse Elizabeth Bennet', she had initiated a correspondence with Colonel Fitzwilliam. There was no doubting her intentions, but that delightful man had become most adept at eluding any traps which might be set for him by one lady or another. Had Caroline only known that any potential bride was measured against Elizabeth – and invariably found wanting – she would have abandoned her efforts long ago. At last, seeing she was making no progress at all, she walked over to her brother until he and Jane should be ready to leave for Stourton Hall, where she was to spend a few days.

In fact, the visit had not been a resounding success. She had hoped that Darcy had made a mistake in choosing Elizabeth to be his wife and that he would realise that she, Caroline, was much better suited to be mistress of Pemberley. It had not taken her long to see how happy they were in each other's company. The pain occasioned by this discovery was only slightly sharper than the one she felt on seeing his exceptionally warm affection for the Gardiners. She had been scandalised when they had been invited to Pemberley while staying at Lambton, but now... from Cheapside to this! A man who actually lived within sight of his own warehouse, a man who was in trade. Really, it was not to be supported. The expression on her face did not induce people to approach her and, aside from Charles, no one took the slightest notice of this haughty yet elegant lady from London. She resolved to return at the earliest possible opportunity and perhaps even cut short her visit to Stourton Hall. When Lady Catherine told her she would be setting out for Rosings that evening with Charlotte and Anne, Miss Bingley offered to accompany them. At first the offer was not enthusiastically received, but then Lady Catherine decided that, since her daughter scarcely talked to her and Mrs Collins did not indulge in gossip, perhaps with Caroline she would be able to catch up with all the scandals then rampant in London. Accordingly, she arranged that they would go back by way of Stourton Hall for Miss Bingley's luggage, which placed the latter under some considerable obligation.

Of course she was not to know that she had handed Lady Catherine the perfect excuse to see Bingley's house, which she could reasonably have no other means of visiting. She even insisted on settling the bill of the inn where they spent the night on their way back! She was recompensed for all this bounty by some mouth-watering titbits about London society with which Caroline regaled her, no doubt adding not only salt but a great deal of pepper, as well.

It has to be admitted that with the departure of Lady

Catherine, her daughter Anne and Miss Bingley, the atmosphere at the wedding reception took on a happier air. Elizabeth was only sorry that Charlotte had been obliged to leave with them, but had extracted a promise from her friend that she would come up to Pemberley with Thomas Quintus while Mr Collins was at a church conference in London. She knew that Darcy liked Charlotte very much but would have been hard put to endure even two hours of Mr Collins, however much Elizabeth assured him that gentleman had improved.

As they were preparing to go on their wedding trip, the young couple bade goodbye to Julian's father and were assured by his brother that he and his wife would be staying at Denton Lodge until the return from the honeymoon. When Georgiana whispered something to Julian's aunt, there was a beaming smile and a warm hug from that lady. After saying their goodbyes to the other guests and expressing their warmest thanks to Darcy and Elizabeth, they entered their coach and drove off.

Much was the speculation as to the destination of the wedding trip, but no one seemed to know. It was no secret to Julian's father. Shortly after the engagement, Julian had asked Georgiana whether she would object to spending all of their honeymoon in England. Given his father's state of health, he was reluctant to go abroad where he could not be assured of a swift return home, should any emergency arise. Perhaps she would agree to Devon or Cornwall? Or the Lake District?

But Georgiana would have none of it. She insisted they tour the immediate area, which was very beautiful, and return to Denton Lodge each night.

One can well imagine how happy her father-in-law was to have them there, but his joy was short-lived. Five days after the wedding, he suffered a heart attack that was to prove fatal. He had made a great effort to be well enough for Julian's sake, but it had all been too much for him. At least he had had the satisfaction of seeing his son married to an exceptional young woman and knew that the family future was in safe hands.

Julian now inherited not only Denton Lodge but also his father's baronetcy, conferred on him upon his retirement from the Bench. Sir Julian and Lady Winslow immediately took up their duties not only on their own estate but also in various ways in the local community. Georgiana soon found that in helping others she could forget her shyness and in time, she even displayed considerable talent as a hostess and chatelaine. Invitations to their dinner parties were eagerly sought and she furthered her husband's career by her genuine interest in other people. She had the knack of making others feel and believe that what she most wanted was to hear all about their aspirations – and their plans for the future. The result was that very soon, Julian would have more clients than he could accommodate!

Elizabeth had, from the first, known that Georgiana would succeed in her role as helpmate to her husband. Her fierce loyalty to those she loved would carry her through any hesitation she might have regarding her abilities. As for Julian, he was to rise even further in her estimation. One day, she asked him about the plantation in Virginia and how it had come about that his father had purchased property so far afield.

'My father had no hand in it, Elizabeth. The fact is that one of my mother's ancestors was among the first settlers there – in 1607. Of course, land was plentiful and he bought a great deal of it. Much later the house was built and cotton was planted, a wise choice of crop, as it happened. Then one day, it was decided that one branch of the family should stay and the other return to England. It was not easy to develop this land: the winters are severe and the summers unbearably hot. I was there for a year, so I speak from experience. A few weeks ago, I resolved that, as they had endured so many hardships over the years, it seemed unjust to be sharing the profits. To come to the point, Elizabeth, I signed over to them my part of the property and waived all claims. We have more than enough for ourselves and any family we may one day have. Georgiana agreed with my decision, and it has given me a great deal of satisfaction.'

Yet another gesture that spoke volumes!

The future was seen to smile on these three happy couples. The Bingleys had been at Stourton Hall just under a year when their twins were born. These they named Julian and Fitzwilliam. Mr and Mrs Bennet welcomed the news of their first grandchildren and Mary was exceedingly proud to have become an aunt with so little inconvenience to herself.

Kitty, by this time married to a doctor and living in Oxford, was not to be outdone and soon informed her parents and her sisters that little Mary was the happiest baby in England!

In all conscience, the Darcys could hardly let the matter rest there and when their first child was born, they felt their happiness was complete. However, the following year Charles Edward Fitzwilliam was joined by Elizabeth Jane, who immediately became the apple of her father's eye.

In due course, the Winslows also trod the path to parenthood and the christening of their first son took place in the church where they had been married three years previously. The late judge's name having been Charles, it was not surprising that the child was christened Charles Fitzwilliam Darcy. His three godfathers were, of course, Bingley, Darcy and the colonel. Georgiana had no doubts about her future. Here she was, together with a healthy baby boy and the six people she loved best in all the world. Yes, her happiness was now complete.

Jane and Elizabeth paid occasional visits to their parents, who were always asked to stay at their respective houses whenever a christening was in the offing. It would be superfluous to remark on Mrs Bennet's first arrival at Pemberley and at Stourton Hall. On her return to Longbourne, she went on at such length that even Sir William Lucas, normally the soul of courtesy and forbearance, excused himself on some pretext or other. It goes without saying that once Mrs Philips was given the news, it spread through Meryton like wildfire.

Mr and Mrs Bennet continued to live at Longbourne for quite some time and for a while Mary stayed home to keep her mother company. However, she had never indulged in gossip and eventually tired of all the snippets of scandal Mrs Bennet was determined to impart, spending more and more time in her beloved library. The day she was able to inform Bingley that she had just finished the Z was the proudest in her young life. From that time on, she even endured the famous nerves with which her mother favoured her.

The Wickhams' life became predictably erratic. Lydia's love for her husband largely outlasted his own for her. His drinking and gambling continued unabated, but later on his tendency to womanize started to alter Lydia's attitude towards him. And after all that had happened, even she did not have the temerity to write to Elizabeth and Jane to complain. For some time now she had been forced to admit that there was little goodness and no integrity in her husband and even his looks no longer compensated for the present humiliations. She stood by him as long as she could, but when he began to flirt openly and brazenly with the wives of fellow officers, she felt that enough was more than enough. She returned home to allow him time to consider what he would be losing if she were to leave him for good. This, did she but know it, was Wickham's greatest punishment. He had thought that, if he stayed married to a wife who was plainly visible, there would be little likelihood that these casual romances could result in an entanglement of any kind.

His judgement was, as usual, flawed. One day, he simply went too far and, as a consequence, was challenged to a duel by a fellow officer. Having no Lydia to put some rein on his drinking, he arrived at the appointed hour in a lamentable condition. True to his nature, he determined not to show how he felt. He would overcome this situation as he had so many others in the past. Even his seconds did not realise there was a problem and the outcome was only to be expected.

The only mourners at his funeral were Lydia, her parents and his commanding officer, aside from his seconds. Mary did not attend since she felt it would be hypocritical to pay her respects to a man she had detested from the moment she first set eyes on him. It had not helped his case that he spoke disparagingly of Darcy and Bingley whenever he could.

It has to be admitted that Mrs Bennet was glad to have her favourite daughter home, even at such a cost. Mary was now free to visit her three sisters. While staying with Kitty, she made the acquaintance of her brother-in-law's cousin, a most delightful teacher by the name of Mark Brooks. They had much in common, for by now Mary really was knowledgeable. She accepted his proposal on one condition: that her library be part of the arrangement. In this way, matters were settled most amicably and, as far as Mark was concerned, she could not have brought with her a more splendid dowry!

Meanwhile, in Kent, peace reigned supreme for Charlotte and her little boy. Her husband had finally placated Lady Catherine, but had rejected Mr Bennet's suggestion of standing by Darcy. After all, Rosings being rather nearer than Pemberley, his situation would have been untenable. Besides, standing by Darcy would have implied some sort of acknowledgement from that gentleman. As Elizabeth's best friend, Charlotte was always treated with the greatest courtesy by Darcy. She could not help but notice his abrupt change in attitude whenever Mr Collins loomed on the horizon. So she told her husband that he had made the right decision.

Lady Catherine spent her remaining years miserably. Since she did not at all care for children, she very seldom paid visits to Pemberley or Denton Lodge, but spent her declining years more and more alone. Her daughter, Anne, had finally succumbed to her illness at the age of thirty-eight, but Lady Catherine refused to be completely isolated and was reduced to inviting ladies she had known in her youth to stay with her at Rosings Park. For some of these it was not too unhappy an arrangement, since, due to advanced age, they had become a little hard of hearing (Lady Catherine had taken to speaking in a rather loud voice). In any case, she continued to ask rhetorical questions, which required no answer of her friends.

There were also others for whom life had not taken a happy turn. Caroline Bingley had decided that spinsterhood was not so much to her liking. At the age of thirty-five (she was six years older than Charles and two years older than Louisa) the extent and amiability of her female friends and acquaintances had somewhat diminished, because they no longer trusted her. She had taken to flirting outrageously with their husbands, clearly in an effort to prove that her charms were still irresistible.

But a fate worse than death awaited Caroline. The only proposal to come her way – and she was now becoming desperate – was from a cloth merchant from Bradford. A very wealthy merchant, it must be said, but a merchant nevertheless. Rather than endure any longer the sneers that she could detect from certain ladies, she accepted him, swallowing her pride in the process.

Mr Hurst, who was an even greater snob than Caroline, was adamant in his refusal to receive them in his home. This was, of course, an excellent excuse to be inhospitable yet again. Louisa, who could not countenance the idea of being estranged from a sister of whom she was exceedingly fond, would stay with her at Bradford for several weeks a year – though not, of course, during the London season. This absence of hers was a very happy time for Mr Hurst, who was then free to stay playing cards at his club without having to be home in time for supper.

Caroline declined repeated invitations from the Bingleys to visit them with her husband. They lived too near Pemberley and she feared that, should the Darcys call on them unexpectedly, which was highly likely, it may cause some embarrassment. She had so often expressed her abhorrence for anyone who was in trade that she feared Darcy might either snub her or cut her dead. In this, she showed how little she understood that gentleman; for he would no more have stooped to such a denigrating gesture than he would have sung an operatic aria.

As a matter of interest, Bingley had spoken to his brother-in-law of Mr Danforth's having amassed his fortune in the most honest way possible. He was thus held in respect not only at Bradford but also in London, where he owned a splendid town house and where Charles and Jane had stayed for a few days. Although it may be said that Charles, with his easy temper, could make friends effortlessly, in fact Mr Danforth was also an extremely pleasant man and the two were most compatible.

On hearing this account of their visit from Jane, Elizabeth reflected that perhaps Mr Danforth was the loser in that marriage.

Meanwhile, in another part of the country, Colonel Fitzwilliam was promising himself never to marry unless another Elizabeth could be found. However, matters were abruptly taken out of his hands by the sudden death of his brother, who had remained a bachelor and had not taken his responsibilities with any degree of seriousness. In fact, even his death showed a certain element of recklessness. At the end of a particularly boisterous party at a Venice palazzo, he had leapt off an upper terrace into a waiting gondola. Unfortunately for him, the gondola was waiting in the wrong place and he was killed.

There were, of course, no children to inherit, so the earldom now came to the colonel. He had perforce to choose a bride in order to carry on the title, which dated from Tudor times.

By some miracle, he made the acquaintance of a very lovely and spirited lady, whom he married and with whom he lived very happily indeed. And three sons made secure the perpetuation of the title.

Mrs Gardiner had once declared Derbyshire to be the best of all the English counties. Elizabeth now knew that her aunt had not overstated matters. When, twenty-five years after she had married Darcy, her uncle retired, there was no doubting where they would choose to settle for the rest of their lives. A delightful house was found for them near Pemberley, at their own insistence, for Darcy and Elizabeth had repeatedly pressed the Gardiners to come and stay with them for good.

By this time, all four of their children were happily married and living in as many counties. They paid regular visits not only to their parents, but also to the Darcys, the Bingleys and the Winslows.

Christmas at Pemberley became a source of great joy not only for the Darcys and their children, both of whom had made very handsome marriages, but for the growing Bingley family and the Winslows and their brood.

The Gardiners were, of course, always welcome, and one day, when they were dining alone with the Darcys, Elizabeth said to her aunt, 'We owe so much to you both. I have often thought how very fortunate it was that you did not have so much time at your disposal, all those years ago. And I recall how disappointed I had been that we would not be visiting the Lake District!'